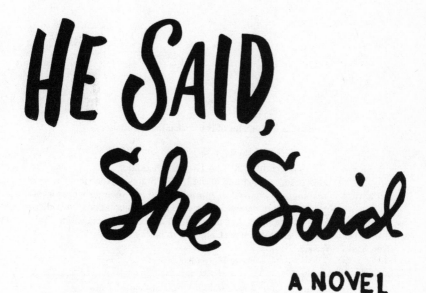

HE SAID, She Said

A NOVEL

by

KWAME ALEXANDER

Amistad

An Imprint of HarperCollinsPublishers

Amistad is an imprint of HarperCollins Publishers.

www.epicreads.com

Library of Congress Cataloging-in-Publication Data
Alexander, Kwame.
    He said, she said / by Kwame Alexander. — First edition.
        pages   cm
    Summary: "When a popular football playa and ladies man and the smartest
girl in school lead a school protest, sparks fly as their social media–aided
revolution grows"— Provided by publisher.
    ISBN 978-0-06-211896-7 (hardcover bdg.)
    [1. Protest movements—Fiction.   2. Love—Fiction.   3. High schools—
Fiction.   4. Schools—Fiction.   5. African Americans—Fiction.]   I. Title.
PZ7.A37723He 2013   2012043496
[Fic]—dc23   CIP
                                                                    AC

Typography by Michelle Gengaro-Kokmen
13 14 15 16 17 LP/RRDH 10 9 8 7 6 5 4 3 2 1
❖
First Edition

*"The future belongs to young
people with an education and the
imagination to create."*
—President Barack Obama

*"I want a person to come into my life
by accident, but stay on purpose."*
—Adele

To my Book-in-a-Day students,
especially North Charleston High School,
whose voices inspire mine

OMAR

"Why does your grandmother put plastic on the sofa, dawg? My butt is itching and sweating at the same time." This is the main reason we don't watch TV at Willie Mack's house. Plastic on a couch. Who does that?

"Then sit on the floor, B. She's trying to keep the couch from getting dirty," Willie Mack says.

"Well, she ain't doing a good job, 'cause it's dirt all up under this joint," I say, and lift up a torn piece of the plastic. "Whoa! B, tell me I didn't just find a fifty-year-old Froot Loop."

1

"She need to go green and recycle this ish," Belafonte says, tearing off a dangling piece of plastic.

"GoGreenRecycle. OhSnap! That'sSomeFunnyIsh," Fast Freddie says, talking as fast as he runs.

"Save the planet, Miss Mable. Save. The. Dayum. Planet," I add to a barrage of laughter.

"IHopeYouDon'tBringNoBroadsUpHere. TheyMightGetCut." We laugh, 'cause we've all bled on this frickin' couch.

My phone buzzes, but I don't answer it. I know who it is, and so does everybody else.

"YouHittin'ThatTonight,T-Diddy?" Fast Freddie asks.

"C'mon, son" is all I say, because everybody knows that's a stupid question.

"Bong bong!" says Belafonte.

My girl, Kym, won't let me touch her hair when we're kissing. "Not my weave, T-Diddy; please, not my weave!" But she loves it when I place her hands on my chest, melts when I blow on the back of her neck. And tonight, after the party, there's a strong wind coming on. Believe that!

For real, though, I must be off my game, 'cause we started talking right before Thanksgiving break, and it doesn't usually take me a whole month to bong bong! I even had to buy her a Christmas gift. Those sterling silver bangles cost me forty-eight dollars. She better be worth it, especially since she's number twenty. Real talk, since I moved down here from Brooklyn, I've smashed nineteen girls—one from the college. It's not even like the girls down south are easier than up north, it's just the perks of being the star quarterback on the state championship football team. Not to mention, T-Diddy looks goooooooooood.

"WhatTimeWeLeavingForThePartyT-Diddy?"

"It's the end of the game. Sit back. Chill, Freddie. Pass the bag." The game we're watching is the shaky-cam video that Willie Mack's mom made of the state championship. The painful plastic-covered couch we're sitting on in Willie Mack's living room is his grandma's. And the bag is roasted sunflower seeds, my favorite.

"How many times you gonna watch this, T-Diddy? Let me tell you how it ends. You throw it to Fast Freddie, he catches it, dodges three linebackers, and runs—"

"C'mon, son, stop hating 'cause I didn't throw you the ball. I can't help it if Freddie is faster than you." Willie's last name is Howard, but that joker is built like a Mack truck, so we call him Willie Mack. It doesn't matter whether he's playing defensive end or tight end, he will hit you, run you over, and never look back. Hit and run, real talk.

"AndBetterLooking." Me and Fast Freddie dap each other.

"Willie Mack, did your moms get the part where that fat-ass left tackle tries to slam T-Diddy at the end of the game?" Belafonte says, then grabs my bag of sunflower seeds from Willie Mack.

"And then you hurdled that woadie like *what*!" Willie Mack says to me, laughing.

"ThatWasClassicT-Diddy."

"If the refs didn't get there sooner, might have been a good old-fashioned West Charleston–Bayside rumble, real talk," I add. I don't even know when the rivalry began, but I know it's crazy intense. At one of the games before I came here, I heard, most of their whole school wore referee-style shirts and flashed fake dollar bills, trying to say that we only win because we pay off the referees. Last year, somebody from our school graffiti-painted their bus during the game. Those jokers were pissed to the highest level of pisstivity when they saw the big Panther on the side of their bus. That joint was classic!

"IfWeSeeThemJokersAgainIt'sOn!"

"Can I please get my seeds?" Fast Freddie hands me the almost-empty bag. These jokers are greedy. "Now y'all shut up and let me watch this." I fast-forward the game.

"Hole up, T, stop right there," Belafonte hollers. "That's the halftime show. I don't want to start nothing up in here, you know, on your grandmother's freezer-bag couch, Willie, but I know he didn't just skip the best part of the game."

"FreezerBag. What!" Fast Freddie laughs it up.

Belafonte is the drum major in West Charleston's marching band. Before T-Diddy arrived, they were the talk of the town, the numero uno, the *primo luciano*. Their rep was unchallenged, unstoppable. Still one of the best bands in the south, but T-Diddy put the gridiron on the map. Now, football rules. Believe that.

Belafonte's cool and all, but if he wasn't Fast Freddie's cousin, I wouldn't be hanging with him. Don't get me wrong, he goes hard. That Katrina tribute they did last year to Lil Weezy's "Tie My Hands" was straight gangsta. They got like 200,000 hits on YouTube.

They have cheerleaders and dancers, but nobody really pays attention to them, especially when the band starts high-stepping. I can't really get with the uniforms—feather plumes and capes and whatnot—but they do bring down the house fo' sho. But, like I said, they no longer run West Charleston. T-Diddy does. So no, I won't be stopping to watch the marching band.

My phone buzzes again. Dang, Kym. I'm coming.

"How you gonna be late to your own party?" Willie Mack asks.

"Next year, when I'm playing for Miami in the Sugar Bowl, maybe you'll be the state player of the year, then you can be as early as you want for your wack party."

"Maybe y'all will get an invite to the Toilet Bowl, 'cause y'all squad be getting flushed every Saturday."

"OhSnapHeSaidTheToiletBowl."

"C'mon, son, you know T-Diddy at the U is gonna change all that. Peep the plaque on my wall at the crib: SOUTH CAROLINA'S MR. FOOTBALL. Recognize."

The only thing I love more than girls, and sunflower seeds, is football. When I was in New York, our team won a lot of games, but I wasn't getting any real love. The Apple is a hoops town. Down south is where football reigns. But it wasn't even my idea to leave New York.

Some kid tried to steal my MetroCard one day after school. He pulled a knife out, but I punched him before he could even think about using it. I got arrested, but the charges were dropped since I was just defending myself. On the way home from the police station, my dad says to me, "If you're young, black, and male in New York City, chances are you're either on your way to jail or coming back from it." After Mom finished crying, she told me it was going to either boarding school in Connecticut or down south. That was two years ago.

I was hoping to live with my cousin Jerome in Atlanta, but when we Skyped that joker, he sounded drunk, looked high, and started bawling like a baby over his missing cat, Roberta Belle. Apparently she'd crawled through an open window, while he was working. At the strip club. I didn't have a problem with it, but Mom was like *hells naw.*

Next, Mom asked me if I wanted to stay in Orlando with her sister, who worked at Disney World. As a clown. C'mon, son.

Finally, Pop called his mother in Beaufort, South Carolina. Grandma told him that his brother Albert had just bought a big place in Charleston.

Uncle Albert is the coolest uncle in the world. When I was little, he'd give all the kids envelopes with cash for Christmas. Before the motorcycle accident, he used to host the annual Smalls family Christmas football classic. We didn't play touch football either. That woadie was hard-core.

When Uncle Albert agreed to let me live with him during the school year, I was amped, until he told me I couldn't bring Muppet. That was a deal breaker for me. We ain't been apart since Dad brought him home from animal rescue like five years ago. But my options were limited. I miss that dawg.

Uncle Al also made me promise I'd attend Howard University, his alma mater. Mom said, "Yeah, whatever, Al," even though she and Pops were sure I was going to Syracuse, like them.

Funny thing is, I'd decided in the seventh grade where I was playing college ball. The minute after I saw Ed Reed, Clinton Portis, Jeremy Shockey, and the rest of them Miami ballers storm Nebraska in the Rose Bowl, I knew I wanted to be a *Hurricane*. I know they kinda fell off lately, but T-Diddy is bringing back the funk and the noise to the U. Plus they got some beautiful waters down there. And a bunch of beautiful women swimming in them. *Holla!*

"Okay, here it comes," I say, turning up the volume. "T-Diddy's about to show y'all why he's Mr. Football."

"Kym texted you like thirty minutes ago."

"Shhhhh! She ain't going nowhere."

"BeCarefulSheMightBreakUpWithYouAgain." Kym breaks up with me like every other day over something stupid. Then she's all up in my face the next day. She needs so much damn attention. If it wasn't for that colossal booty, it'd be deuces.

"Good, 'cause her birthday is next week, and I really

don't want to have to get her nothing."

"SheGetsNuskins."

"Pass me them sunflower seeds and pay attention," I tell them.

We watch the last play of the last game of my high school career. State championships. West Charleston High vs. Bayside High. And even though I've watched it like a million times, I want to see it a million more.

Fast Freddie lines up on my right.

I yell, "Red-23-4-17-23-hut."

I hand off the ball to Willie Mack. He tosses it back to me. Flea flicka.

On my left, I glimpse a six-foot, three-hundred-pound monster charging at me like he hasn't eaten in days. And T-Diddy is dinner.

I dodge out of his way. *The Matrix.*

I Peyton Manning that joint. Throw a perfect thirty-yard bullet to Fast Freddie.

The entire crowd at West Charleston High School jumps to their feet and yells. . . .

Claudia

"'Touchdown' by T.I. is okay," I say, slipping out of my sweatpants, "but how about we do something a little classier?"

"Whath abouth Christh Brownth?" Tami squeals, the day-old silver stud in her tongue making her sound like Mike Tyson. Or a pigeon. Or Mike Tyson talking to a pigeon. With a lisp.

"Eminem and T.I. ripped it on 'Touchdown,' but a Chris Brown song would be hella nice," Eve translates. "What y'all think?"

"I was thinking we should add a number with a strong message," I add, and all the girls, except the freshman twins who agree with everything, smack their teeth.

"Girl, why you always talking that message stuff? This ain't the Civil War movement," Eve yells, and the rest of the girls laugh.

"You mean the civil *rights* movement," Blu, the captain of the dance team and my best friend since West Charleston Montessori, corrects her.

"I *mean* we got the Battle of the Bands next month, and Belafonte said there's forty-five seconds at the beginning of the show for us to do something. So we need to add a fresh routine. Represent for West Charleston with a brand-new Panther dance. Something real fly," Eve adds.

"Well, let's take a vote," Blu says, "at practice on Monday. Now, who's ready to par-*tay*?"

"I need a drink for real. Whose dumb idea was it to practice over Christmas break anyway?" Eve asks, looking at me.

Saying Eve and I don't get along too well is like saying that there's homeless people in New York. Freshman year, we used to be tight—me, her, and Blu—until she told everybody that Blu was a lesbian. It wasn't that big of a deal to Blu, because she didn't and still doesn't care what anybody thinks. But for me it was nothing short of evil betrayal.

"You *are* coming to the party, aren't you, Claudia?" Blu asks, ignoring her. "The whole dance team is coming."

I've danced since I could walk. Two things my parents made me and my sister do since we were little: go to church and take dance lessons. Since they've been doing missionary work, we haven't really kept up with the church tradition, and the truth is, I've been bored with dance ever since I discovered words.

Freshman year, when I started writing for our school paper, the *Panther Pride*—back when it used to be a real paper—I told Blu I wasn't going to try out for the dance team. She got all upset, yadda yadda yadda, and practically guilted me into it. The best thing I can say for it is it keeps me in shape, and it looked good on my college application. Hanging out with these girls in practice is drama, though. And hanging out with them after practice, well, that's trauma. For real.

"Nope, too much work to do."

"Girlth, youth canth doth that shith thisth weekendth," Tami says. Eve shoots the twins a mean look when they start to giggle in unison.

"Actually, we need to finish tonight, so it can be edited tomorrow."

"Come to the party. Enjoy yourself before school starts on Monday. I'll help you after," Blu says.

"Girl, I want to, but I'm still working on that piece about the arts budget cuts the school board proposed."

"Can't wait to read that thrilling piece of journalism," Eve says. "You ought to be writing an exposé on the football team and how they beat Bayside for the state championship. *Whoop whoop!* And make sure you post lots of pictures of my girl Kym's dude, T-Diddy." T-Diddy is the West Charleston quarterback who led the Panthers to victory against the powerhouse Bayside Tornadoes. He's also the resident ho at our school. I did not stutter.

"Ith knowth thatth righth, girlth." She high-fives Eve.

"For real, nobody cares about arts funding and budget cuts. Do something on them rappers who got caught robbing banks. Now, I'd read that ish." Eve laughs.

"You won't be laughing if the funding for our dance team gets cut."

"Maybeth youth couldth doth somethingth onth girlsth gettingth knockedth upth andth havingth abortionsth."

Blu and I look at each other, but not at Eve, who we both know had an abortion last year. Trifling.

"I read that the school board has, like, a six-million-dollar deficit," Blu says, trying to quickly switch subjects.

"What paper did you read that in?" I ask.

"I read it on Cruella's Facebook page."

"Are you serious? Dr. Jackson has a Facebook page. O frickin' MG!"

The only way I can figure that Dr. Brenda Jackson got the principal job at West Charleston High School is that they required someone who a) never smiled, b) hated teenagers, and c) bathed in a vat of perfume every morning before she came to school to torture us. Ugghhh!

"Claudia, she's got like a thousand friends. She's always posting pictures of all her crusty puppies," Blu adds.

"Sheth tweetedth abouth ith tooth."

Tweetedth. "What's that?" I ask.

"For somebody who got accepted to Harvard early, you sure don't know ish. It's called Twitter," Eve says, smacking her teeth all the way to the shower. "You need to come out that cave."

"Ignore her. So just come to the party for a minute, and then we'll go do your work."

I nod to Blu, because I know she's not going to take no for an answer. She never does.

"Plus, my mom just got a new pair of Louboutin red bottoms that will go perfect with those skinny black jeans I gave you for Christmas. Can you say diva!"

"Really, our principal is on the Facebooks?" I ask, still dumbfounded.

OMAR

Tdiddy Smalls is Panther till I die baby. Just rolled up to the after-party. Poppin' that Polo collar. Now 'bout to pop them bottles. LOL.
Like · Comment · Share · 24 minutes ago ·

👍 **Willie Mack**, **Freddie Callaway** and 9 others like this.

It's not Brooklyn, but it'll do. Music is blasting from some-body's iPod. More girls than guys. Kids from all over the county show up. Tonight is special, 'cause the whole Panther football team is up in here celebrating. So when three guys from Bayside's losing football team show up in the front yard, loud and drunk, things get a little out of hand.

"Y'all ain't Panthers, y'all is cheaters," the fat guy who tried to slam me in the championship game says.

"Big Moose, these cheaters think they actually can beat us," a guy I recognize as their quarterback says to the fat dude named Moose. That's appropriate.

"T-Diddy, am I mistaken, or did we whoop that Bayside ass?" Willie Mack hollers.

"Panthers swooped down and wrecked shop, forty-one to thirty-five," I boast.

"Everybody knows the officials liked y'all better than us; helped y'all win," Moose says.

"IfY'allWeren'tSoUglyTheOfficialsMightHaveLiked Y'allToo."

"Who you calling ugly?"

"You, Bayside busta," I taunt, using some of my Brooklyn slang on them.

"WhatKindaWackNameIsTheBaysideTornadoes?"

"I got your *wack* right here," the quarterback says. Two more of their guys start gritting on us even harder.

"We're Tors, and we can finish what y'all started on the field right now," Moose says, looking dead at me.

"Y'all ain't Tors, y'all is toys. 'Cause you got played," Willie Mack adds. We laugh loud as hell, not because it was that funny, but to show solidarity.

Ten of our teammates come running out of the party. Now what? Apparently, Bayside is not as stupid as they look. They back away, speeding off in their green hoopty, but not before screaming, "Watch your back, Titty."

"Them boys is wildin' out. They drove two hours just to talk ish," Willie Mack says.

I hope so. Them kids from Bayside be acting foul. Somebody got shot outside their school last summer.

"Let's go get our party on," I say, and we head back inside.

"Let'sGoGetOnThemFigLeaves," Fast Freddie says.

"You need to leave that stuff alone. You know the NCAA got drug testing," I remind him. Clemson wants him *baaaad*, but his priorities are a little wack.

"Where's wifey?" Willie Mack asks me as we walk back into the party.

"Upstairs taking a leak. We out when she comes down. It's going down tonight, fellas!"

"IKnowThat'sRight. KnockItOutTheBoxT."

"Believe that, and tomorrow, it's on to the next one." Fast Freddie and I laugh alone, 'cause sometimes Willie Mack gets all righteous.

"Sometimes that ish is foul, T-Diddy."

"Willie Mack, you know how T-Diddy do. Love 'em and leave 'em, hit 'em and split 'em. Use 'em then lose 'em, baby!" Now he's laughing too.

"I don't blame you, T. Your girl Kym is legit, but—"

"But what, Mack?"

"No offense, T-Diddy, but Claudia Clarke is the bomb dot com," he says, his mouth mopping the floor, his fingers pointing to the sofa. "She's wearing them jeans like she painted them on."

"*That's* Claudia Clarke, the one who's always collecting ish for kids in Africa and whatnot?" I ask, eyeing the baddest chick at the party. She looks like a cross between Beyoncé and, uh, Beyoncé.

"Last week she was collecting shoes for needy kids. Soles4Souls."

"SheThinkShe'sHarrietTubman." Fast Freddie is my dude, but sometime he says some real stupid ish.

"Dayum, homegirl doesn't dress like that in school. I knew she looked good, but not *that* good."

"You know she's in the band," Willie Mack says.

"HalfTheSchoolInTheBand."

"For real, what instrument?" I ask.

"A dancer."

"She's out there twirling the batons and whatnot?" I ask.

"She'sADancerAndAGoody-Two-Shoes."

"I ain't know she was packin' all that. She got butt for weeks," I add, still checking her out.

"MondayTuesdayWednesdayBadunkadunk."

"I'd hit that in a heartbeat," Belafonte says, popping up out of nowhere like he always does, drinking something pink and questionable.

"Me too," I tell him.

"Too fly for you, playa," Willie Mack says.

"What's that, Mack?"

"You married to Kym, pardner," Belafonte says. "Plus, she's been checking me out at band practice. That's all *me* over there."

"SheDon'tDateHighSchoolGuys."

"C'mon, son. She ain't never met T-Diddy, aka Ladykilla, aka Honeydipper, aka Pantydropper."

"TDiddyBeDroppingPantiesLikeIt'sHot!"

"Trust me, cuz, it'll never happen. She's Oprah. You're Flavor Flav," Willie Mack says, dapping Fast Freddie and sending Belafonte to the floor, bowled over with laughter.

"Good luck with that, T. She only dates college dudes with GPAs of four-oh or higher," Belafonte says, then leaves as fast as he came.

"MaybeHalfOfMeCanDateHerThen," Fast Freddie adds, laughing.

"Willie Mack, I know you ain't doubting T-Diddy's playa skills."

"I'm just saying, they may work on some of these other nasty girls, but not her."

"BongBong," Fast Freddie says. "Don'tForgetThe-T-DiddyThree-StepGuaranteedLadykillerPlanOnHowTo-BagAGirl."

"Straight out of the playa's playbook," I throw in, sending me and Fast Freddie into a fit of laughter.

"Yeah, well, I bet you fifty dollars you can't get her number," Willie Mack chides.

"A phone number? Hah! Make it a buck fifty, and I'll bring you her panties."

"OhSnapT-DiddyGoesInForTheKnockout. Whatchu-GonnaDoMack?"

"Bet!"

Watch this," I tell them. "If you see Kym come down, give me a warning." I spit out my sunflower seeds, pop in a peppermint Altoid, and jet over to Beyoncé, who right about now, got me almost *speechless*.

"Lips like yours ought to be worshipped/I ain't never been too religious/But you can baptize me anytime," I say to Claudia, and kiss the back of her hand. Some girl I smashed last month hears me, rolls her eyes, and walks away.

"You trying to flirt with my girl, T-Diddy?" Blu, who

lives around my way, screams from her seat across from us.

"Naw, Blu, I was just telling her she's rockin' those black jeans," I say, still smiling like a kid on Christmas morning. During the awkward silence, I see Fast Freddie and Mack looking in our direction, trying to see if I still got my playa moves. The moment also gives me the chance to survey her curves, imagine my fingers dancing inside her waist-length hair. "Don't hurt your eyes," Blu screams, while Claudia's still using silence as her shield.

"Can I at least get a smile? You know the poem was dope." She's giving me no play. "You probably already know, but I'm T-Diddy."

"T-Diddy, huh?"

"Yeah, can't stop, won't stop."

"Do you always speak in clichés?"

"Only when I'm spellbound. You want a drink?"

"I don't drink."

"Yeah, me either."

"So why'd you ask?"

"You got T-Diddy flustered."

"And *T-Diddy* has me bored."

"Oh, it's like that, Claudia Clarke. Even after I wrote that haiku for you."

"First of all, it wasn't a haiku. And second, you didn't write the poem."

Busted! Step one of the T-Diddy Three-Step Guaranteed Ladykilla Plan: unsuccessful. "A'ight, a'ight, you got me. I got it from a poetry book. I was just trying to impress—"

"That's sad, Omar."

"So you do know T-Diddy?"

"Again with the annoying third person."

"I'm just saying."

"No, you're not."

"No, I'm not what?"

"No, you're not saying anything. Nothing. I'm sure you're a nice guy. And I appreciate you taking the time to come over and introduce yourself, but we're about to leave."

"Why so early? We're just about to do T-Diddy's Panther Shuffle."

"Sorry, never heard of it."

"It's easy. Like the cupid shuffle, but T-Diddy puts more bounce in it. Feel me?"

"You steal poems and dances, huh?"

"Don't hate, participate."

"Thanks for the cliché. Gotta run. We have articles to write," she says, and turns to her friend Blu McCants. "Time's up, Blu. Let's go."

"Oh, so you write for the *Panther Pride*. That's what's up. Make sure you do a piece on the team. We can even talk later tonight. I can give you an exclusive interview," I say, smooth as butter.

"Look, I don't want to be rude, but I'm not interested in boys, especially ones with girlfriends. So keep it moving, Mr. Football."

"Me and Kym are just good friends," I say to her, intent on getting a phone number and texting her tonight.

"Oh, I see. Well, good thing, because Kym, your, uh, good friend, is headed over here right now."

I spin my head around so fast I almost get whiplash.

"What's going on over here?" Eve, standing next to Kym, asks, smacking her lips.

"Nothing—we were just talking about an article she might do on me," I jump up and answer.

"And I was just leaving," Claudia adds.

"Oh, 'cause I hope you weren't trying to push up on my dude," Kym says, waving her hands a few inches from Claudia's face.

"Eve, check your girl. Don't nobody want her 'dude.' Let's go, Claudia."

"Nobody asked you, Blu. Stay out of this business," Eve counters.

"Trick, Claudia is my business."

"I bet she is," Kym says sarcastically. "Don't let us hold you up. I'm sure you got a big night planned." She and Eve laugh, and I know I better do something before this ish goes sideways.

"Kym, this is all a misunderstanding. Claudia, T-Diddy appreciates the love. Can't wait to see the article. We out." I grab Kym by the waist and we head outside. I grit on Willie Mack and Fast Freddie as I pass by. Them jokers think this is funny, I bet.

"Omar, what were you and Claudia Clarke talking about in there?" Kym asks as I take her hand in mine and head toward Uncle Albert's pimped-out van, wondering if she overheard me and Beyoncé talking.

"Uh, nothing, she's a—"

"A dancer, I know. And I'm your *good friend* now, huh?" She snatches the hand with my forty-eight-dollar silver bangles away.

"Cat got your tongue? Speak up, Omar," she says, then leaves with Eve, aka Evil.

Deuces! You'll get over it.

Back at the party, Tami comes up to me.

"T-Diddyth, myth parenths ainth hometh—"

"I'm good, Tami. I'll holla," I interrupt. Been there and

done that when we kicked it last year. These beezies is treacherous. I make my way over to Mack and Fast Freddie.

"Where's Kym?" Mack says, trying not to laugh, and drinking some of the suspicious pink concoction. "So how'd it go?" he asks.

"That was foul. Why didn't y'all warn me?" I ask.

"BetterStepUpYourGame,Playa."

"C'mon, son, my plan is guaranteed. You know how T-Diddy gets down."

"Stick to football, 'cause you struck out, homie," Mack says, now full-blown laughing. "Pay up, cuz."

"It ain't over yet. Trust me on that. I'm not finished with Miss Claudia Clarke. I still got two more steps."

"The bet ain't forever, cuz. You got one month."

"A month? C'mon, son. T-Diddy doesn't need a month."

"Way out of your league, son," Willie Mack adds, laughing.

"TakeTheMonthWoadie. IHeardSheDon'tLikeFootball PlayersEither."

"It's not about what she likes. It's what she needs. And that kitty needs a Panther. Believe that!"

Claudia

pantherpride.com

Panther Star Is Player of the Year

by Blu McCants

As we all know, in December, Freddie Callaway's dazzling one-handed catch from star quarterback Omar Smalls sealed the state championship game against Bayside, for the 10–2 Panthers. Omar Smalls, aka T-Diddy, was voted South Carolina's Mr. Football, which is given to the state's most valuable player of the year. When asked about his achievement, T-Diddy responded, "Football is my life, so this award means everything to me. As I prepare to play college ball, I just hope my legacy here at West Charleston is all about WINNING!"

Click here for additional articles on the Panthers.

West Charleston High Makes Top Ten

by Claudia Clarke

Don't get too excited, Panthers. This isn't good news. For the second year in a row, our school has made the Association of Secondary Schools' (ASS) list of the ten worst schools—violence, teen pregnancy, and low academic achievement. We have the highest teen pregnancy rate in the United States. Seems like the girls at West Charleston High School (WCHS) are carrying more than just backpacks these days. Many are carrying babies. School principal Dr. Brenda Jackson says, "We're looking at ways to combat it. Right now these girls are having sex when they don't want to. They just don't know how to say no."

This is not an issue that we can just sweep under the rug, Panthers. Our friends' dreams are being shattered by unplanned pregnancies and abortions. Girls, we have to treat our bodies like the sanctuaries they are. Stop letting guys sweet-talk us. Start respecting yourselves and demanding respect. There are eighty-seven pregnant girls at our school. Ask yourself, are those numbers you can live with? I sure can't.

Rap Bandits Caught

by Blu McCants

Police are no longer on the lookout for the notorious rap bandits. Last month, authorities found an iPod Mini owned by one of the robbers on the lobby floor of the Coastal Carolina Bank and Trust (CCB&T). In December, two masked men robbed the North Charleston branch of CCB&T. Authorities say this holdup had the same modus operandi of two other branches that were robbed in 2008 and 2009: Two men, one carrying what appeared to be a gun, walked into a CCB&T and proceeded to pass a note to a teller demanding money. They then made the bank managers strip to their underpants while apologizing to the customers/hostages for causing the economic recession. After locking each bank employee in the vault, they escaped in an employee car, which they abandoned in the driveway of a local foreclosed home. I guess truth is stranger than fiction.

The robbers, most definitely hip-hop fans, always wear masks of old school rap groups: Salt-n-Pepa, Eric B. & Rakim. In an interesting departure, during the most recent bank robbery, the thieves wore masks of two of the most iconic rappers of all time, hated rivals—both of whom are dead—Tupac and Biggie.

Police found the iPod on the floor near the bank teller who was targeted. During the investigation, police listened to the iPod Mini and discovered a playlist consisting of a demo tape recording by one of the bandits, who mentioned his name more than fifty times on one song. Police captured both suspects, who have not been publicly identified, on Wednesday.

Eleventh grader Tami Hill was conflicted about the whole situation. "I mean, I don't condone any type of thievery, but only God can judge them. I love Tupac's music, and Biggie was just juicy. It's good to see that they squashed their beef and they're working together, even if it is, like, robbing banks. Get money!"

"LOL! Blu, you crazy. Tami is dumb."

"Claudia, it took me two hours to translate her tongue-ring gibberish."

"Take that mess out of there," I say, and we just laugh and laugh, like it's not three a.m. and my sister's not trying to sleep.

Our e-newspaper staff is small. As in me and Blu. I try to focus on the hard-news stuff, while Blu likes writing the light, quirky, fun pieces.

"I know. Can you believe she actually said that mess?

Hi-frickin-larious! You finished yet, Claudia? I'm tired."

"Yeah, I just need to find a quote for my piece on the budget crisis."

"While you're doing that, I'm going to set up your Facebook page."

"I'm overwhelmed with anticipation."

West Charleston School Board

by Claudia Clarke

Being a member of the Panther Pride Marching Band, I know we all like a little drama. Well, if the school board doesn't stand up for us, it will be the end of all the drama, journalism, visual arts, and our award-winning band here at West Charleston. Sources say that the state funding reductions will cut arts funding in our schools by 68 percent in the West Charleston school district. If our governor truly cared about education, our futures, she wouldn't let this happen.

In a letter on the state's website, she says, "The economy has hit us hard in South Carolina. It requires us to tighten our belts. Unfortunately, that means we will see some dramatic decreases in state funding for extra-curricular school activities. Each school district will have to figure out a way to manage this challenge." Since when is creative writing "extracurricular"?

Ironically, our very own school board couldn't figure out how to close the funding gap and save the arts, but they managed to find the money for a new football stadium, which will cost almost four million dollars. I don't know about y'all, but we should use some of that money to keep our arts programs alive. Maybe our school is failing because sports are more important than academics.

The school board did not respond to our emails. Neither did the superintendent. Blu McCants, captain of the dance team and a senior headed to study communications at the College of Charleston, had this to say: "I love what our football team has done for our school, and I am proud of them. But do I think that they are more important than the band or the drama club? NO." Read more.

OMAR

Usually I get a ride home from Willie Mack after weightlifting, or I catch the bus. But Willie left early today, and I left my wallet at home. So it's just me and my big dogs.

Along the way, I always run into these annoying little kids selling sweetgrass baskets. It's cool, and a lot of tourists buy them—we even got some placemats and whatnot around Uncle Al's house—but don't be harassing me every time I walk by. I'm just sayin'.

"NO!" I scream at the dirty little joker who tries to sell me a flower made out of grass. Take a bath.

When I get home, Uncle Albert and his two buddies are holding court on the front steps. Drinking Snapple, eating sweet potato chips, and blasting his favorite music: jazz.

Uncle Al is my man, but for once I'd like to come home after school, eat dinner, and just chill, without a lecture from him and his crew.

"Spooky, 'Watermelon Man' is a song about the African jungle," Al says to Spooky Johnson, who sports long white dreadlocks with a matching beard.

"What's up, Uncle Al," I interrupt. "I worked up an appetite lifting weights. Let me get some of them chips."

"Boy, whatchu know about potato chips?" says Spooky,

"What kind of question is that?" I ask.

"Do you even know who invented the potato chip, boy?" he asks me. These old dudes be clownin'.

"Spooky, you know Smalls don't know nothing 'bout his history. Him a big-time football player," Uncle Al says, handing me the bag of chips.

"'A man who prides himself on his ancestry is like the potato plant,'" Clyfe recites, speaking as usual in random quotes. Sometimes he'll jump off with a poem or something that's dope, and I'll steal that joint, but mainly he says ish that only make sense to him. "'The best part of which is underground.'"

Clyfe who always is acting like he's Confucius, decked out in a neon purple suit and a cream-colored fedora. He looks like Barney, if Barney was a pimp.

Uncle Albert took over the West Charleston Community Facility about three years ago, when the economy crashed. The city couldn't afford to keep the doors open, so he decided to take his lottery winnings—nobody knows how much he won—and turn it into a social, educational, and employment programming facility for people in the community who got it rough. Actually he doesn't call it a facility anymore. He calls it a clubhouse. And he renamed it the Library of Progress.

Most folks who come here got bad luck or been laid off from their job. But a few, like Clyfe, just like to hang around a lot, straddling the crazy fence. Spooky used to live in the basement with his sister and her husband, who doesn't like bathing. I still don't go down there. I stay on the third floor, in the loft.

The Library of Progress has helped a lot people. The clubhouse doesn't require health insurance or money. "Just a desire to love and be loved" is what Uncle Al likes to say. I wish they had a desire to clean up after themselves, 'cause I'm sick and tired of scrubbing floors and toilets on weekends. I give Uncle Al his props, though—he's doing good stuff.

Every evening, the three of these jokers reminisce about the good old days. Back when they were marching and protesting for civil rights. Either Clyfe's quoting Gandhi or Martin Luther King, or Unc and Spooky are telling me stories about their rallying days at Howard University. I act like I'm listening to them, since I know they just a bunch of old dudes hanging on to their past because the future is creeping 'round the corner.

"Boy," Spooky lectures, "that there potato chip you just put in your uninformed mouth was invented by George Crum, an African American/Native American chef at a restaurant in Saratoga Springs, New York, in 1853."

"Oh, snap! Why didn't you tell me these chips were that old?" I say, laughing and spitting the chip on the concrete.

"Nephew got jokes," Uncle Al says to his buddies.

"Boy, I know I told you before, but that was one helluva game y'all won. Whipped Bayside like they was runaway slaves," Spooky says.

"'Slaves lose everything in their chains, even the desire for escaping from them.'"

"That's my boy. His mama and them think he's going to Syracuse like they did, but Smalls is going to Howard, right, Smalls?" Before I can lie, Spooky jumps in.

"Donovan McNabb played at Syracuse. You do kind of remind me a little of McNabb."

"He doesn't look nothing like McNabb, Spooky. That boy

throws like Manning and runs like Vick," Uncle Al says.

"But don't be messing round with them dogs like Vick, boy. End up in jail," Spooky adds.

"More black boys in jail than in college," Clyfe says, making sense for the first time in a while. And then he messes it all up. "Kafka said, 'All knowledge, the totality of all questions and answers, is contained in the dog.'"

"Shut the hell up, Clyfe," an annoyed Spooky shouts.

"Watch the verbal, Spook," Uncle Al says, enforcing his no-profanity rule on the clubhouse premises.

"When is the big announcement, boy?" Spooky asks.

"My coach has scheduled it for next week. You coming?"

"As long as you don't choose Howard. Though I heard their volleyball team is the bomb," Spooky says, and laughs.

"Hater! Smalls, don't sleep on Howard. We got decent sports, but when you become a Bison man, you become a real man. I remember this one time a bunch of us from Howard went up to New York for a protest. We were marching over the Brooklyn Bridge, chanting, 'We're fired up, can't take no mo'! We're fired up, can't take no mo'!' When we got to the other side, the police unleashed them dogs on us—" and I know that's my cue to get ghost, 'cause another one of his long-ass stories is coming, and I got to Skype

Mom and Pops, finish my trig homework, then call Kym to see if she's still mad at me.

Tdiddy Smalls is now single.

Like · Comment · Share · Monday at 10:30 pm via Brizzly

👍 Freddie Callaway, Tami Hill, Belafonte Jones and 27 others like this.

> **Freddie Callaway** Deuces!!!!!!!
> 9 minutes ago via mobile · Like

> **Savannah Gadsden** :-(
> 9 minutes ago · Like

> **Willie Mack** Y'all be back together tomorrow. Watch!
> 9 minutes ago · Like

> **Freddie Callaway** On to the next one. Bwahahahahaha!
> 9 minutes ago via mobile · Like

> **Tdiddy Smalls** Fo' sho
> 8 minutes ago · Like

> **Tami Hill** She won't right for you anyway. T-Diddy needs a ride or die chick.
> 8 minutes ago · Like · 👍 4

> **Leah Rivers** I'll be the new lady in your life. LOL. Call me.
> 7 minutes ago · Like

Tdiddy Smalls Too late.

7 minutes ago · Like

Freddie Callaway Beyoncé?

7 minutes ago · Like

Tdiddy Smalls Fo' sho. Plan's already in action.

7 minutes ago · Like

Freddie Callaway She look more like Rhi Rhi to me.

6 minutes ago · Like

Belafonte Jones Who dat? Claudia?

6 minutes ago · Like

Tdiddy Smalls C'mon, son, no names.

6 minutes ago · Like

Tami Hill She always acting stuck up.

5 minutes ago · Like · 👍 4

Belafonte Jones HATER!!!!

5 minutes ago · Like · 👍 2

Savannah Gadsden T-Diddy, you really know Beyoncé?

4 minutes ago · Like

Freddie Callaway ROTFLMAO

4 minutes ago · Like · 👍 7

Leah Rivers **SMH**

4 minutes ago · Like

Tdiddy Smalls I'm out, y'all.

4 minutes ago · Like

Leah Rivers Congratulations on being Mr. Football, T-Diddy

4 minutes ago · Like · 👍 10

Blu McCants Go Panthers!

3 minutes ago via Friendly for iPad · Like · 👍 2

Tdiddy Smalls @Blu Tell your girl, she's Bonnie, I'm Clyde.

3 minutes ago · Like · 👍 4

Belafonte Jones BONG BONG!!!

3 minutes ago · Like

Blu McCants I told her and she said you're corny and she's tired.

2 minutes ago via Friendly for iPad · Like

Willie Mack You just got canceled, homie. Like a bad sitcom. LOL.

2 minutes ago · Like

Tami Hill Anybody watching The Game? It's on BET right now. OMG! This show is sooooo good.

1 minute ago · Like

Freddie Callaway Bwahahahahaha!

1 minute ago · Like

Willie Mack T, you cooking good eats for bkfast 2morrow?

1 minute ago · Like · 👍 4

Tdiddy Smalls @Blu I'm patient.

1 minute ago · Like

Blu McCants Good luck with that!

Less than a minute ago via Friendly for iPad · Like

Tdiddy Smalls C'mon son. T-Diddy don't need luck. It's my destiny, child . . . LOL.

Less than a minute ago · Like · 👍 32

Claudia

Tdiddy Smalls wants to be friends.
West Charleston, South Carolina
Blu McCants and 2 others are mutual friends.

"Please don't tell me you thought I'd fall for that," I tell him, laughing out loud. "You'll have to do much better than that, Omar."

"No, no, you got T-Diddy all wrong. I wasn't looking where I was going, and I, uh—"

"Where were you going?"

"To Spanish class."

"That's back the other way, amigo. You should at least organize your lies. Here's your picture," I say, handing him back the tattered black-and-white of him in diapers and no shirt.

"So, whatchu think? Cute, right?"

What I think is: lame. Bush league. Amateur. The most popular, and supposed "coolest," guy in school is trying to get at me, and the best he can think to do is "accidentally" drop his baby picture at my feet. So random. Did he really think I was going to pick it up, see how cute he was, and confess my undying love and lust for him?

The funny thing is, even if the picture was adorable, which it isn't—okay, maybe it is, just a little—I still wouldn't give him any play. Omar Smalls is only interested in droppin' panties, and I'm not about to become his next victim, no matter how cute he was as a baby. Look at that watermelon head. LOL.

"Yeah, real cute. But why is your head so Brobdingnagian?"

"T-Diddy doesn't know what that means."

"I'm not surprised. Maybe T-Diddy should look it up."

"Maybe T-Diddy will."

"Stop speaking in third person. Ugghh!"

"Go out with me Friday night, and T-Diddy will."

"Again, not interested."

"If you're still worried about Kym King, we broke up."

"Yeah, I heard. Still not interested."

He throws his long arms in the air, not like he's fed up—which *I* am—but more like he's reaching for something.

"Uh, what are you doing?" I ask him.

"Raising my hands to the constellation. The way you look should be a sin, 'cause you my sensation. Claudia, tell me what I got to do to be *that* guy?"

"First, be original." Now he's biting off *Kanye*. "Second, read. Third, change your whole identity and get a purpose and a plan besides trying to get between as many legs as possible." He just stares at me with that diamond stud blinging from his ear. What, no comeback? I close my locker and head to the library to drop off a book. Don't follow me, please.

"Oh, sorry. I didn't see you," Eve says, bumping into me and knocking my books on the floor. I know you did that ish on purpose.

"Whatever," I say, and bend down to get my books.

"Hey, T-Diddy, what's really good," she says, giggling. I guess he did follow me. Jeez.

"Keeping it really hood. You know how T-Diddy does it."

Ugghh! I stand and turn to leave.

"Walk me to class—I got a message for you," she says, and rolls her eyes at me.

"Yeah, do that," I say, and head toward the library.

"I got to run, Eve. I'll holla," I hear him say. Leave me alone already.

The sign on the library surprises me: LIBRARY CLOSED.

"What the?" I say.

"What's wrong?" Not-Kanye asks me.

"Read the sign," I say.

"How is the library closed? That joint is always open," Omar says.

Duh!

I totally ignore him and make my way to my first class so I can find out what the heck is going on. The bell rings, so I don't expect him to still follow. Wrong again.

"Mr. W, what's up with the library being closed?" I ask, walking into class.

"Yeah, Mr. W, what's the dill, pickle?" Omar asks, laughing.

"I'm afraid the lumpenbourgeoisie is at it again," Mr. Washington says, as only Mr. Washington can say it. I wonder if he talks like this to Mrs. Washington, at home.

"The lump who and the what?" Omar says, and some of the kids in class laugh.

"Mr. Smalls, shouldn't you be in your class?"

"Fo' sho, Mr. W, but I just wanted to make sure Claudia

got to class." I roll my eyes at him. "Seriously, what happened, Mr. W?"

"The school board passed the mayor's arts funding cut legislation," he tells us. "Dr. Jackson suspended the drama guild, the poetry club, the choir, and the marching band, and several teachers and staff have been laid off or reduced to part-time, including the librarian."

"They fired you, Mr. W?" Omar hollers

"Not yet, but the writing's on the wall. We're all walking on eggshells," Mr. Washington answers. "As for the library, it'll be open on Mondays and Fridays. Ms. Stanley will split her time between two schools."

"This sucks," Omar adds, trying and failing at sincerity.

"Preposterous," I say. "What about those of us who study in there?" I roll my eyes at Omar. "And need to check out books?"

"I was sad because I had no shoes, until I met a man who had no feet. So I said, 'Got any shoes you're not using?'" Omar says. I turn around, and he's got this stupid smile on his face. I hate how his upper lip curls when he smiles.

"Really, a joke?" I say, not looking for an answer and hoping he'll just leave.

"What? T-Diddy was just trying to lighten the mood.

My uncle Al says that it's better to stop crying to keep—I mean, uh, to laugh to keep from crying, and whatnot."

Uggghhh!

"It's still not fair. Or right. They can't just get rid of our activities and close the library and fire people. We have to do something about this."

"Oh, snap, I just realized he said they sacked the band. B is going to be pissed. What are y'all gonna do during halftime next season?"

"Is everything always football with you?" I ask, getting more frustrated by the minute. He tries to put his arm around me.

"Get off of me."

"I was just trying to console you."

"Console yourself. I bet the money for the new stadium didn't get cut."

"It didn't, but it's not his fault, Claudia," Mr. Washington offers. "You want to blame someone, blame our governor. Blame the school board. Blame our whole community for not taking a stand for what matters most. Words, music, and visual melody. Somehow we've forgotten the power of art to make us better; better students, better parents, better people."

"That's the triple truth, Ruth." Omar's even lamer than

I thought. "Real talk, Mr. Washington," Omar adds, looking at me.

"Don't even act like you know or care about anything but scoring touchdowns. You're a fraud."

"Oh, so now I'm a fraud 'cause I play football. That's ridiculous."

"You're ridiculous." What's even more ridiculous is that during this whole conversation about the well-being, the frickin' future of our school, the other kids in the class could care less. They're in their own little worlds, where the only things that matter are who's wearing what, who's doing who, and who's having a party on Friday.

"Tami," he says.

"Huh?"

"Tami Hill, she's throwing this Friday's party," he says, pumping his fist at the students echoing him.

"Like I said, immature, shallow, fraud."

"Whatever, Claudia. Mr. W, this is an atrocity, and we shouldn't stand for it. Because if we don't stand for anything, we'll, um—"

"Fall for anything," Mr. Washington finishes. "Omar, I never knew you were this passionate about the arts."

"Me either," I add sarcastically.

"The arts are important," he offers.

That's the best you got. Jeez!

"Indeed they are, Mr. Smalls. The arts inspire innovation by leading us to open our minds and think in new ways about our lives."

"I don't know about all that, Mr. Washington, but I just think we need to fight back," he says, winking at me. What a jerk.

Mr. Washington's phone vibrates, and he glances at it.

"I need to take this call. I think a quiz is in order," he says to a slew of Boooos. "Mr. Smalls, thanks for stopping by—now off you go, lad," he adds, walking into the hallway.

"Yeah, be gone, Mr. Small," I say.

"I think we ought to . . . ," Omar says, and then pauses, as if he's trying to figure out what to say next. "Have a protest."

"A protest? You mean like shutting down the school? Who are you, Usher now, trying to 'Light It Up'?"

"Hole up, hole up! Cut me some slack, homegirl. I'm being straight up."

I am so not your homegirl.

"A small protest and whatnot. Real talk, Claudia."

"It would definitely be a very small protest. Just you and me. If it was a free Rick Ross concert, sure. But a protest. Good luck with that," I tell him.

"I got a plan," he counters.

"Omar, I hate to tell you, but nobody cares about the arts funding being cut. The students here are clueless. You're clueless. Why am I even talking to you?"

"My boys were right, you are a stuck-up bi—"

"Go ahead and say it. Show your true colors like the rest of your thug friends."

"For somebody who claims to be a writer, you're the clueless one. I'm just trying to be creative, think outside the box."

"Like there's anything creative about throwing a ball?"

"The Super Bowl is like a movie, and the quarterback is the leading man."

Uggghhh!

"Look, T-Diddy has a master plan. You on board or what?"

"Or what."

"Tomorrow we're going to put on a rally," he says, like it really is a concert. "We're going to galvanize the streets."

"What streets?"

"Look, trust me. Let me call the plays. I got you!"

"No, you don't. But, yeah, we'll see." If there's a chance it'll help save a teacher's job, I'm down. I guess.

"Can I call you tonight, Claudia Clarke?"

"You mean, can you call me a B tonight, like you just did a few seconds ago."

"I'm just saying, if we're gonna do this protest, shouldn't we, uh, you know, uh, discuss the *plan*?"

"Just let me know what time your little rally is, and I might be there."

The way he said plan was suspect. I knew all he wanted was to score with me, like he had with every other girl at West Charleston High School. Thank goodness the bell rang.

"Dang! Mr. W. , since I was here on official biz, can I get a pass?" Omar says to Mr. Washington, who's walking back into the room.

"Don't try me, Mr. Smalls," Mr. Washington says, putting his phone back on the desk.

"So I'll call you tonight, Claudia?" he asks on his way out the door.

His protest idea does kind of intrigue me. Even though he is still a jerk.

"Text me."

OMAR

"You better watch out—I'm coming for that queen," Uncle Al taunts during our nightly game of chess.

"Check," I say, smiling. "I guess you taught me how to play the game a little too well, Unc."

Even though I'm six moves away from checkmating him, my head isn't really in the game.

Fast Freddie and I were trying to lift weights after school. I say trying because his cousin Belafonte was in there, bawling like a broad the whole time because the band got cut. C'mon son, it's just the band.

The deal is, I only got one step left in the T-Diddy Guaranteed Ladykilla Plan. Too bad. I'm making this ish up as I go along. This protest thing might work, though.

First things first. I gots to figure out what to say, so I can text her.

After dinner, I went online to see if I could figure out a plan. First I Googled "protest," which had, like, 413 million results. C'mon, really. Then I tried "rally," which turned up a bunch of information on Rally Software and Checkers Drive-In—their burgers are no joke. I did find some news articles and historical pages on rallies, but I wasn't really trying to read all that. If I was going to impress Claudia tomorrow, I needed an easy plan, and I needed it fast.

"Wake me up when you move." He ignores me. "You know I got homework to finish, right?"

"Smalls, stop rushing me. By the way, we're still going fishing Sunday morning, to celebrate Dr. King's birthday."

"What does fishing have to do with Martin Luther King?"

"Know your history, Smalls. 'Teach a man to fish and you feed him forever.'"

"Dr. King didn't say that."

"Shhhhh, I'm trying to concentrate, Smalls."

It doesn't matter how hot or cold it is, this joker loves to go fishing. And since he's in a wheelchair, this means that I have to go as well.

When we first started going out, I hated it. Sundays are

my sleep-in days. The last thing I want to do is go digging for bait at four in the morning. The messed-up thing is, when we get out there, I do most of the fishing.

There is one upside to it, though. I did discover Folly Beach.

"When is your big college announcement?"

"You know when it is, Uncle Al, now move."

"What time is it? Is ESPN gonna be there?"

"Seriously, Unc, you're going to either move here or there." I show him. "And then I'm going to trap your queen, and then you have to protect your king with the rook, and then I got your queen, and then it's two more moves max until checkmate." I pop a handful of seeds in my mouth and lean back.

"Well, ain't that some ish. Smalls got me up against the wall. You do them dishes yet?" Whenever Uncle Al is about to lose, he goes off on some domestic randomness.

"Yeah, I did the dishes, and took out the trash, and cut the grass. So now what?" He ignores me again. "You give up, old man?" Uncle Al hates losing. But he hates giving up even more.

"Smalls, I told you about spitting those sunflower seeds on my porch. You're going to need to sweep up out here tonight."

"Unc, it's cold out here. Let me do that tomorrow."

Charleston's cold is nothing like Brooklyn's ice. But when it's been seventy degrees for like most of the winter, and now all of a sudden it's in the fifties, that's cold.

"There, I moved." Unfortunately for him, it's the worst move he could have made, 'cause now I can have him mated in two moves. But since it's getting late and I'm on a mission, I prolong his defeat.

"Unc, tell me about one of your rallies from back in the day."

"What do you want to know?"

"Did you ever have to speak at one?"

"Boy, I spoke at about twenty of them things," he says, finally looking up from the board at me. "I remember this one we had at Howard in the snow. I really got them jokers fired up, Smalls."

"What were you saying?" I ask excitedly, taking down notes on my iPhone.

"I started off with a fancy quote, from Gandhi or Frederick Douglass, you know something to get them ready for the funk I was about to bring. Then I just told 'em like it was. The power of the people to change the world. Freedom ain't free. Everybody has a voice. Speak up for your rights, for your children's rights, ya know! Boy, I'm telling you, by the time I finished, it was one hundred degrees out there in December. I'm talking revolution, you hear me, Smalls, we—"

I do hear him. For the next two hours he talks and shouts and moves across the front porch like a Baptist preacher. The neighbors don't mind. They're used to seeing him and Spooky and Clyfe holler like this.

I hear every story he's told me before, only this time I actually listen. *Research.* We never finish the game, and even though none of his sermon makes a whole lot of sense, I have enough stuff to at least text Claudia and show her I'm the real deal.

Omar Smalls: Hole up, hole up. I thought you were going to be doing the speaking.

Claudia Clarke: This was your idea. Plus, I'm a writer, not a talker.

Omar Smalls: Seriously, you expect T-Diddy to speak at the rally. LOL!

Claudia Clarke: I don't even know if I'm coming.

Omar Smalls: This conversation would be so much

easier on the phone, or on Facebook.

Claudia Clarke: The Facebooks blur the lines of friendship too liberally.

Omar Smalls: The Facebooks? Bwahahahaha!

Omar Smalls: Claudia, you still there?

Omar Smalls: Hellloooo! You still there?

Claudia Clarke: I'm here, but GTG. Homework.

Omar Smalls: WAIT!

Omar Smalls: You like my plan for the rally though, right?

Claudia Clarke: Mildly impressed.

Omar Smalls: C'mon, you know T-Diddy did his thing.

Claudia Clarke: We'll see tomorrow.

Omar Smalls: So you're coming.

Claudia Clarke: I didn't say that.

Omar Smalls: T-Diddy bringing the noise and the funk tomorrow, homegirl.

Claudia Clarke: Homegirl? Seriously?

Omar Smalls: That's my Brooklyn coming out. How y'all say it in the country? LOL!

Claudia Clarke: Oh, so now I'm country?

Omar Smalls: JK

Omar Smalls: You are a flower in the ocean.

Claudia Clarke: Good-bye.

Omar Smalls: Can I get a thank-you? Dayum!

Claudia Clarke: For what? Next time, why not throw the sun in your mixed metaphor cliche.

Omar Smalls: W/E. I was just trying to be real for a minute. Let you know I was feeling you. It's all good, though. I ain't trippin'.

Claudia Clarke: Yadda yadda yadda . . . So you're not just into sports, but theater too.

Omar Smalls: Theater???

Claudia Clarke: DRAMA!

Claudia Clarke: You're not slick, Omar. I know what you're trying to do. Like I told you at the party, I don't date athletes, and I don't date boys with girlfriends.

Omar Smalls: Me and Kym broke up.

Claudia Clarke: See you at the rally tomorrow.

Omar Smalls: Yeah, the rally. Why they cut the arts funding anyway?

Claudia Clarke: Because the school cares more

about football and basketball than art and music
and making sure we have textbooks that aren't
ancient.

Omar Smalls: Well, we did win the championship.

Claudia Clarke: And how is that going to change the
world? What impact does winning a ball game have
on changing the human condition, Omar?

Omar Smalls: Changing the human condition? WTH.

Claudia Clarke: Stand for something, or fall for
anything, Omar.

Omar Smalls: Is the sky falling, or am I just high?
Bwahahahahaha!

Claudia Clarke: Everything's a joke to you, isn't it?

Omar Smalls: Buzzkill.

Claudia Clarke: You may not be serious about
about saving the arts in our school, but I am.

Omar Smalls: Hole up, hole up. T-Diddy is still down!

Omar Smalls: I hope you wear them jeans to the rally. Those ones you had on at the party.

Claudia Clarke: Again, random . . . But thanks for the, uh, compliment.

Omar Smalls: Look, we can at least be friends, right?

Claudia Clarke: That's cute, Omar. You want to be my friend?

Omar Smalls: Yep.

Claudia Clarke: How about friends with benefits?

Omar Smalls: That'll work.

Claudia Clarke: T-Diddy thinks I'm bootylicious?

Omar Smalls: Fo' sho!

Claudia Clarke: Let's go out on a date.

Omar Smalls: Word!

Claudia Clarke: Take me to the Avery this weekend.

Omar Smalls: That's a new restaurant.

Claudia Clarke: It's a museum and cultural center.

Omar Smalls: For black people, right?

Claudia Clarke: It's *for* anybody, but it has African American art.

Omar Smalls: I knew that. I was just messing with you.

Claudia Clarke: Whatever, Omar!

Omar Smalls: C'mon, give T-Diddy a chance.

Claudia Clarke: Okay, I'll give you a chance.

Introduce me to Pat Conroy, and I'll let you smash?

Omar Smalls: Oh Snap! For real?

Claudia Clarke: Word!

Omar Smalls: Who's Pat Conroy?

Claudia Clarke: Exactly!

Omar Smalls: Seriously, who is he?

Claudia Clarke: The fact that you have to ask that question means that you will never get in my jeans.

Omar Smalls: I know you all goody-two-shoes and Ms. Valedictorian and whatnot, but you ain't gotta play T-Diddy like that. No need for all that--I'm just trying to be nice.

Claudia Clarke: I see. So you're not trying to play me?

Omar Smalls: Nope. This ain't about you, even though you too stuck-up to see that. I'm trying to help save the band, help the teachers keep their jobs. This is about the people. Freedom ain't free.

Claudia Clarke: And neither is a good piece of ass, apparently. What's it worth, Omar, about $150?

Claudia

Two things you can count on in our school: one, that you will find a pregnancy test in the girls' bathroom, and two, by the end of school, everybody knows who took it. News and rumors spread faster than the bossip at West Charleston. The only way to guarantee that nobody finds out your business is not to tell anybody your business, not even your best friend. I learned that the hard way freshman year.

So it didn't take me long to hear it from Blu, who heard it from Tami, who heard it from her sister, who heard it from her boyfriend, who overheard his big brother, Willie Mack, talking to Freddie Callaway about it on the way to school one morning.

Claudia Clarke: Yeah, I know all about your little bet.

Omar Smalls: What bet?

Claudia Clarke: You're not the first, Omar, and you won't be the last. Like I said, I'm not interested. I got plans, and shallow jocks with no purpose other than to throw a ball don't fit into them. We can't be friends. I'm on a mission, and right now my focus is on taking a stand against the wack school board. So you can either be down with that or keep it moving. Feel me?

Omar and I stand with nine other students on the school's side lawn at seven thirty a.m. Six of them, including Luther, who helped me with the Save the Chimps project, aren't even here for the rally. Apparently we've intruded on their smoke zone.

Before school, at lunch, and after school, the same group of eighteen-year-olds gathers on the side lawn near the picnic tables to smoke cigarettes. A part of me is glad that at least we look like we have a small crowd. The other part of me gags on all the cancer smoke that is going to kill them. And me.

The sweat on Omar's head can't be from the weather. It's not even sixty degrees. He's nervous; in way over his head. He's probably happy that not a whole lot of students have shown up. I guess you won't look like the fool you and I both know you are.

He apologizes to me for the whole bet thing. But like I tell him, "It really doesn't matter. You're a guy. And guys are apes." I'm probably too hard on him, but it is what it is. Guys only want one thing: to get inside our minds, so they can get between our legs. My last boyfriend was a professional primate.

Leo was a sophomore in college. He spoke French, quoted Shakespeare, drove a Benz; and his singing opened me in ways that I'd never been opened. I used to go hear him play guitar and sing on Monday nights at a local coffeehouse. Unfortunately, it was months after I'd given him the lala before I realized that Leo was a frickin' rock star by all definitions—he sang for Lindsay on Wednesday, Dominique on Thursdays, and Tina and Bubbles on Saturday. I haven't dated since.

"Hey, T-Diddy, you wanna toke, man?" Luther says, taking his cigarette out of his mouth and offering it to Omar. When Omar shakes his head, he reaches into his pocket and pulls out option number two, definitely not a cigarette. Omar grins at him, looks at me, frowns, then shakes his head again. If I didn't already have a million reasons not to get to know him, I would now. A jock who sleeps around *and* smokes weed. How cliché can you get?

"Well, we tried, Claudia. No point in staying out here in this nip," Omar says to me.

"What about the teachers, the band, the school's arts funding? What about galvanizing the streets?"

"We can't have a rally with no troops, homegirl."

"I thought you said you were going to get the word out."

"I did. Put it on Facebook. Like fifty people said they were coming. Look," he says to me, pulling out his phone and showing me his Facebook page.

"Hey, look!" Angel, Luther's girlfriend, screams, pointing to the front of the school. Coming from the direction of the buses is a swarm of West Charleston students.

"Oh, snap," says Omar.

"I guess I underestimated you and Facebook," I throw in. "It's on now, Mr. Football."

Within minutes, more than two hundred kids, led by half the football team, fill the lawn in front of us. Five minutes later, most of the school is out here.

"Pass that Bobby Brown," one of the football players yells, the smell of Luther's weed still soaking the air.

"T-Diddy's. About. To. Bring. That. Funk," Blu whispers, sneaking up behind me.

"This should be interesting," I answer.

"Why we here?" a kid from the crowd screams.

"I guess we better do this, Omar. You okay? I only ask because you don't look okay," I say, somewhat mockingly.

"T-Diddy's fine. Let's do this. Introduce me."

"What?"

"T-Diddy needs an introduction. Part of my game ritual. You know, a hype man. Or woman."

"You serious? What should I say?"

"You're the writer," he says, and jumps up on one of the picnic tables, leaning down to give me a hand up. Before she goes off into the crowd, I see Blu taking a puff of one of Luther's cigarettes. I can't tell which one it is.

"Come on, homegirl." He pulls me up. Strong hands.

"It's up to y'all to save the band. Do this thing big, for real," Belafonte screams up at us.

"IsThisSomeKindOfCampaignSpeech?" Freddie Callaway, another football player, yells from the front.

"Isth T-Diddyth runningth forth presidenth?" Tami shouts, and the first couple of rows in the crowd roar because no one has a clue what she said. She's with Eve and Kym, and they're gritting on me like we have beef.

Standing on the table, I shout to get everyone's attention. It doesn't work. I do it again. Same result. Eve and Kym laugh. T-Diddy looks at me and smirks, then mouths, "Let me help you."

"Na na na na!" he yells with his hands cupped around his mouth. Random.

The crowd screams back, "Na na na na!" Then they chant, "Hey hey hey, good-bye." They sing it twice more, and then they stop and applaud. I have no idea why it works, but I'm glad it does.

"Fellow classmates, thank you all so much for coming out this morning," I say to the almost silent crowd. I say almost, because I do get a few boos. Okay, maybe a lot. "Some of you may know that the arts funding has been cut in our school. Well, today we are going to take a stand for what's right." I can feel the sweat trickle down my back and forehead. Why are you nervous, Claudia. Jeez! Now I'm stuck. Now more kids are booing. I have no idea what to say next.

"Hole up, hole up! This is your boy T-Diddy. All homegirl is trying to say is our school is in trouble." Omar apparently has an idea. "We lookin' bad, y'all, real bad. Our school is one of the worst schools in the country for two reasons:

one, they don't care about us, and two, we don't speak up for ourselves."

"Preach, T-Diddy," a kid in the back of the crowd yells, and everybody laughs. I'm surprised they're actually listening to him.

"How many of y'all take art?" About fifty kids raise their hands. "How many of y'all take theater? Who's in the gospel choir?" It seems like most of the hands go up. When he asks, "Who's in the marching band?" cheers and barks fill the air. Belafonte throws his fist in the air and gets the crowd high-stepping. It's not *like* a pep rally. It is one.

"Well, T-Diddy and homegirl want to school you on something: the governor of our great state and the school board have cut the arts funding, so ain't gonna be no more marching band or music class or school plays or gospel choir. Feel me!" The boos and shrieks from the crowd are loud and angry. We have ourselves a rally.

Omar continues, "But we don't have to accept this. They don't want us to survive, it's a setup, but even if you're fed up, guess what?"

Seems like everybody in the crowd screams, "KEEP YOUR HEAD UP!"

Tupac, really? Jeez.

"Panthers, look up at the sun. Do you know what that means?"

"It don't mean it's summer. Hurry up with your speech, cuz. It's chilly," a kid screams from the back of the crowd. Everybody, including me, laughs at that one.

"True! It also means this: the sun illuminates the head, I mean, the eye of the man, but it shines into the heart, I mean, it shines on top of . . ." Omar fumbles, looking at me for help. I shrug because I have no idea what he's doing.

He continues, "I mean, the time is now for us to speak up. The sun is telling us to shine, to speak up now. We must all be the *sun*. BE the sun . . . yeah, that's it: BE THE SUN, AND LIKE THE SUN . . . WE WILL, WE WILL, WE—"

"What we gonna do, Omar?" asks Luther, who along with the other smokers is now as amped as the rest of us.

"We will do, uh . . . nothing," he finally says.

Blu and I look at each other like WTH! I shoot Omar a look of puzzlement and rancor. Seven hundred apathetic kids in West Charleston finally got excited about something other than football, parties, and sex, and this fool tells them to do the same thing they've been doing all along: *nothing*.

OMAR

Did I really just say "nothing"? I'm so busted! Claudia's giving me the crooked eye. Not like I had a chance with homegirl anyway. I can't believe Willie Mack and Freddie opened their mouths. That's some foul ish. And now I'm standing up here looking stupid over some lala. Ain't nobody saying jack. They're just staring at me.

I can't wait to get out of here. Five more months till Miami. T-Diddy had the crowd fired up. I was sounding good for a minute, though. Claudia checking me out, smiling. Why is it so damn quiet out here? Somebody say something. Claudia, say something. I helped you out, you could return the favor, Miss Stuck-Up. But you're probably too good for that.

T-Diddy ain't going out like this. I'll just be quiet too, like Gandhi. Yeah, T-Diddy about to be Buddha up in here. LOL!

Clyfe was talking about Gandhi the other day. What's that quote he was saying? Something like, "In silence the soul finds the path." Or "the light comes through the attitude of silence." Something like that. Wait a minute! Oh, snap, I'll quote some of that Gandhi ish. Watch out, T-Diddy is about to bring the noise.

"Y'all heard T-Diddy. We ain't doing nothing," I repeat. "In our quietness, we will find the light." I look at Claudia, and she has the same baffled look as the rest of the students. I wink at her. Am I getting inside your head yet, homegirl? "Time to galvanize the streets," I whisper to her.

"Well, you better galvanize them quick, because first bell rings in five minutes," she says back to me. I had forgotten about the time. I look at my phone. We've been out here for twenty-five minutes.

My adrenaline is on super charge. It's like I'm back on the field, down a score, with less than a minute left on the clock. I can read the defense. The blitz is coming on strong from both sides. The center hikes the ball, I drop back, fake a handoff to the fullback, run to my right, there's a big joker coming hard for me. I reverse to my left, there's two more charging full speed. I look down-field, see Fast Freddie sprinting toward the goal. I pump fake a pass to him, and the animal on my right stops, turns, just long enough for me to dodge around him. I'm running this ball. Willie Mack throws me a mean block. T-Diddy's going in for the touchdown. Oh, yeah, I'm about to score, Claudia Clarke.

"What do you mean, we're doing nothing?" Blu screams.

There are more rumblings from the crowd. Kids are getting restless.

"I mean, today Dr. Martin Luther King would be like seventy, if he were alive." Homegirl holds up seven, then eight fingers. *Close* enough. "Let's honor him by taking a stand, Panthers." The crowd goes wild. I yell at the top of my lungs, "We're fired up, can't take no mo'. We're fired up, can't take no mo'. We're fired up."

"Can't take no mo'," the crowd chants.

"We're fired up."

"Can't take no mo'," they repeat.

"It means that today at eight fifteen a.m., in protest of all the problems here at West Charleston High School, like, uh, filthy bathrooms—"

"*Yeah*, and nasty lunches!" a kid yells.

"Ancient textbooks . . ." Claudia tries not to smile,

but she can't help herself. "The ridiculous ban on school dances . . ."

Wild applause from the students. I'm starting to feel this protest rally thing.

"But most importantly," I continue, "T-Diddy stands before you about the arts funding being cut. This is the last straw. We're fired up, can't take no more!" More loud cheers.

"This morning, when everyone's in class. At eight fifteen, right after the tardy bell rings, repeat after me: WE. WILL. ALL. BE. QUIET. For ten minutes. Holla if y'all hear me!" Piercing yells. "A'ight, quiet down, quiet down . . . this is what we gonna do. At the beginning of first period, nobody says a thing, for like ten minutes. Until they listen to what we want, to what we need to change our condition, there's nothing more to say. Feel me."

The warning bell sounds, which means we have like three minutes to get to class. The crowd disperses, chanting, "We're fired up, can't take no mo'."

I help Claudia down from the bench. "What do you think about your boy now?"

"I think if you're going to be using other people's words, you ought to learn the actual quotes."

"Oh, you got jokes. Don't hate 'cause T-Diddy brought that Gandhi fire!"

"For a minute I thought T-Diddy was about to go up in flames," she say, trying not to laugh, and failing a little. She's a tough nut to crack.

"Shows how much you know about the nonviolence movement. Dr. King, baby!"

"It's an interesting plan. I hope it works," she responds.

"T-Diddy always plays to win."

"Well, we better get to class."

"Should we meet after school to, uh, debrief?" I say, smiling and hoping she gets my hint.

"Good-bye, Omar."

"Good-bye, Beyoncé," I mouth as she walks away in black jeans that barely make it up her waist. I was so caught up in the rally, I hadn't even paid attention to the jeans. Oh, snap, she wore the jeans.

"The best thing you never had," Willie Mack says, sneaking up behind me.

Claudia

The best part of the whole thing was that for once it felt like we were one school. We weren't the guys and the girls; we weren't the cool and the callow; we weren't the athletes and everybody else. For ten beautiful minutes, we were one united school, one aim, one silent majority.

When the bell rings at eight fifteen, Mr. Washington, our comedian government teacher, begins calling the roll backward for no other reason than he thinks it will amuse us. It doesn't. By the tenth name, he looks up to see if in fact all ten are absent. They aren't.

To be fair, our class, like most classes at West Charleston, is prone to bouts of terrible behavior—talking on the phone during class, teacher pranking, and lots worse. But today, for once, we sit in our seats, attentive and focused. The look on his face isn't one of surprise, but sheer bemusement at our antics.

"I see it's going to be one of *those* days, people," he remarks. After taking a sip of his organic apple cinnamon tea—Mr. Washington is a self-proclaimed organic nut—he resumes the roll call in his best Bill Cosby imitation. Only he sounds more like drunk Bill Cosby. It takes everything under the sun not to laugh at that.

By the twentieth name, it is apparent he's given up on us—and his humor—when he pounds his desk, jumps up from his seat, and shouts "So nobody's here? Okay, then maybe you should be in ISS." He pulls out his infamous pad that he uses to write students up, mainly the same three kids in the back of class, for in-school suspension. There are slight rumbles, but nobody speaks. "Last time, people," he continues. "Claudia Clarke, don't tell me they've coaxed you to the dark side." I just look at him and shrug.

Ironically, we've been studying about civil disobedience in his class. From the Roman Empire to the civil rights movement to Occupy Wall Street, we've studied centuries of nonviolent resistance. And here we were practicing our own form of it, with Omar Smalls as our very own Dr. Martin Luther King, Jr. *Not!* He just got lucky. His silent protest seems to be working, at least in Mr. Washington's AP Government class.

"Mr. Washington, like, may I see you for a moment, like, now?" says Ms. Morgan, the giddy English teacher with the permanent smile painted on her face.

"Sure, give me a minute." He picks up a stack of papers on his desk and hands them out. "Well, you don't have to talk to take a pop quiz." The widening of eyes and arms thrown into the air signify our collective moans and groans. Mr. Washington then grabs his tea and joins her in the hall.

I feel bad that I didn't warn Mr. Washington about the protest. Omar said it probably wasn't a good idea if we told any teachers, for fear they might try to shut us down. First thing he said that I agreed with.

A couple of kids hole up four fingers to indicate how much time we have left. I look at the clock on the wall. Eight twenty-one. I start answering the twenty-question pop quiz. This silence is foreign to me.

In my four years at West Charleston, I have never been able to hear the sweet sound of the birds outside our windows, let alone hear myself think. But this morning the black-bellied birds are loud and lovely. Why can't all mornings be like this? Minus the stomach growls from the guy behind me, who apparently skipped breakfast.

When Mr. W comes back in, at eight twenty-four, he doesn't look as puzzled. He takes a sip of tea and speaks to us in his best British accent, which is also his worst.

"It appears that whatever has taken hold of you is contagious. Ms. Morgan's sophomore class is giving her the silent treatment as well. Bollocks."

The clock reads eight twenty-five, and a collective gasp consumes the room, like we've all been underwater and now we've risen to the surface.

"Mr. Washington, we're fired up, can't take no mo'," says Belafonte.

"Yeah, you should be proud of us, Mr. W. This is straight democracy in action," Blu adds.

"Claudia, give me the four-one-one on all this democracy in action hullabaloo," Mr. Washington says.

"They're right, Mr. Washington, we're taking a stand. The students at West Charleston High School are no longer sitting idly by while our school slides down the academic gutter. You can try to take our band and our library and our drama and our teachers away, but you can't take our souls. And our souls will never let the powers that be take the arts from us. Our souls are on fire, Mr. Washington."

"And we're gonna burn this mutha down if we have to,"

screams one of the troublemakers from the back.

"Metaphorically, of course," Mr. Washington says.

"What did Ms. Morgan say to you?" Blu asks.

"Well, she'd gotten wind that some kind of senior silent prank was going to take place, so she just gave a quiz in her class. But no one talked in her class. Is this a schoolwide thing?"

"We are not a prank or a thing. We are a protest," Belafonte says defiantly.

"Well, good for you, Mr. Jones."

"This is a movement, Mr. W," Blu adds.

"The students of West Charleston want our arts funding reinstated, and today's silent protest was to let our voice be heard," I say forcefully, and realize I am now standing up. Mr. Washington starts clapping, like he's just seen a good play.

"Bravo, bravo! Well done. What you've just done is more than any government class taught by a handsome organic vegan can teach you." He's back to trying to be funny and failing miserably. "Give me those quizzes back. A's for everyone. Let's watch a movie."

Well, we weren't silent after that announcement. He may not have been too funny, but right then Mr. Washington pretty much guaranteed that all of us would be voting for him to win WCHS Teacher of the Year for the third straight year.

Sitting there thinking about the teachers who got laid off, and the library being closed, it dawned on me that our little protest probably wasn't going to get their jobs back, any more than Dr. King's March on Washington ended racism and poverty. That reality was further cemented in my mind when I went to talk with him during the movie.

"Hey, Mr. W."

"Claudia, whose idea was this silent treatment?"

"Believe it or not, Omar Smalls's."

"Omar 'T-Diddy' Smalls?" he asks in disbelief.

"Yes, sir."

"Well, good for him," he says, smiling.

"What kind of idiot school board doesn't think we need books? What kind of school has a library that's only open two days a week?"

"Our school isn't failing; we're failing our school. I'm afraid West Charleston is turning into a twenty-first-century prison of mediocrity."

"Well, the inmates are taking over, Mr. Washington." This puts a smile on his face.

"Have you given the principal a list of demands? Has anyone called the school board? What do your parents say about this? What are the next steps? What's your plan?"

Demands. School board. Plan. Huh? We don't have any of that; at least, I don't think Omar does. We're just trying to bring attention to the funding cuts. Next steps? That sounds like homework. Which is the last thing I need on my already full plate—physics, English lit, French, trig, AP Government, and the *Panther Pride*.

"Ms. Clarke, you're a smart student. Don't let the sun catch you sleeping." What's up with all the sun metaphors? Jeez!

"I don't quite understand, Mr. Washington."

"The night's the time to close your eyes. Your soul may be tired tonight. But tomorrow in the morning light, there's work to be done. So don't let the sun catch you sleeping," he sings.

He strums an invisible guitar to go along with his horrible singing. After he takes the last sip of his tea, he goes back to turning the virtual pages of the book he's reading on his iPad.

I'm not sure what Omar has in his mind, other than trying to run game on me. But I'm the activist, and I don't need him to keep this movement, uh, moving. Wake up, Claudia. This is a whole lot bigger than raising a few dollars to save chimps.

Maybe I'll just convince him to help me a little more. He did get the students to come out to the rally. Yeah, I'll just string Mr. Football along until the protest gets some legs. Then I'll cut him loose like the stray dawg that he is.

OMAR

"BeTheSun," Fast Freddie says, laughing. "ThatWas-ClassicT-Diddy."

"Don't sleep. T-Diddy got plenty of tricks for these tricks," I say, even though my fake ladykilla plan failed, and there's nothing else up my sleeve but a thirsty ego.

"Where's my money, dawg?" Mack says, holding out his hand.

"C'mon, son, if y'all ain't talk that ying yang about the bet, I'da been all up in that. Fo' sho!"

"T-Diddy, that was tight," says Leah, a cheerleader I used to get with, from a nearby table.

"That silent protest was tight, T-Diddy. My teacher canceled our test," another kid says, walking past me.

"Let me get some of them fries, Mack," I say, snatching the whole bag before he can grab it.

"Dude, don't make me jump over that table," he says, standing up like he wants some of this. "Gimme my joints back."

"Why you wildin' out like them Bayside boys?" I hand him back the bag of fries, now half empty. He's scowling like I stole his wallet or something.

"Why you shooting daggers, Mack? I'll get you some more fries. Dayum!"

"For real, son. I saw two of them Bayside boys at the mall last night. They was muggin' me hard. Watch out for them jokers, T."

I ain't scared of them fools. Believe that! I steal one more fry.

"That's foul, man."

"MakeWayForT-Diddy'sFans," Fast Freddie hollers.

"For real though, them jokers in my class was quiet for like the first time since birth," Willie Mack adds. "Yo, Fred, what is B doing?" We all look in the direction that Willie Mack is pointing and see Belafonte holding up a sign that says TELL THE MAN TO SAVE THE BAND!

"ThatWoadieGotAPetitionToKeepTheMarchingBand," Fast Freddie answers.

"Is it that deep, really?" I ask, even though apparently it is. He's wearing his band helmet and cape and whatnot.

"HeFinallyGotDrumMajorAndNowTheyShutHim-DownBeforeTheBigBattleOfTheBands," Fast Freddie says. "He'sSoSeriousHeMightBurnThis JointDownFor Real."

"I guess I was wrong about you. Nice job! Are we doing it again?" Blu comes up to me and asks.

"Where's your girl? I haven't seen her since the rally," I say.

"Probably off saving the whales or something. You know how she does," Blu answers. "Here, she told me to give you this." She passes me a folded note and walks away. What are we, in third grade? Still, the anticipation owns me.

Before I can open it, a pair of soft hands covers my eyes from behind, and I wonder, no I hope, they belong to homegirl.

"Guess who, baby?"

"Who?" I ask, but when I hear those forty-eight-dollar bangles clanging, I know exactly who it is.

"It's me, baby," Kym says, rubbing my dome.

"What's crackin', Kym King?" Willie Mack says.

"Willie, I saw your baby sister pictures on Facebook. She's so precious," Kym says.

"That's my niece. She's cute, right?" Willie Mack pulls

out his phone to show me and Fast Freddie the pic, but we just look at him like, really?

"What up, Kym," I say, partly disappointed and partly galvanized by her superminiskirt and the water balloons she rubs against me.

"You baby, that's what's up. The whole school is buzzin'. I didn't even know you was into that kind of stuff."

"Shoulda stuck around. A lot you didn't know," I say.

"I'm here now. How about you let me find out tonight?"

"BongBong!" Freddie mouths. Willie Mack is still trying to show us photos.

Why not? She's only offering what she promised me. Thing is, it's my night to cook dinner. Last time I skipped dinner, Uncle Al made me dust the whole house.

I guess the rally did work. I'm getting what I want, even if it's not from who I want. Oh, well, different chick, same thing. T-Diddy ain't choosy. Claudia Clarke playing way past hard to get anyway. Got to keep it moving.

"That's cool. We'll celebrate your birthday early," I say, and take her fries. She blushes, kisses my forehead, then leaves to join the other cheerleaders outside. She used to be one, till she got kicked off for beating down a cheerleader from Independence.

"T-DiddyHereComesYourOtherGirl." I turn around,

and here comes Claudia Clarke in that pair of bangin' jeans.

"Willie Mack, let me see those pictures," I say. When Claudia Clarke gets to our table, I put on a show. "Awwww, she's so beautiful. A precious little thang," I add.

"Still trying, I see," Claudia says.

"Check out the pictures and the video of my niece," Willie Mack says, handing his phone to Claudia. "Ambrocious."

"OnlyInTheCountry."

"You mean Ambrosia," I say, hoping, for the child's sake, he mispronounced it.

"Nope, it's Ambrocious." Fast Freddie almost falls out of his chair laughing. I would join him if homegirl wasn't standing over me. "My sister's name is Amber, and her baby daddy's nickname is Ferocious."

SMH!

"Aww! She's so cute, Willie Mack," Claudia says, handing his phone back. "That's just sad, Omar. Trying to use your boy's niece to impress a girl."

"Naw, it wasn't like that, I was—"

"Yadda yadda yadda. Look, save your energy. I'm not your type, homeboy. You're looking for shallow water; I'm an ocean."

"ShallowWaterWow!"

"You sure do smell good as the ocean. What's that you're wearing, DKNY?" I say, letting her know T-Diddy got a little class.

"Soap. You should try some," she responds.

"You still got jokes." As we talk, I slowly walk toward the hallway, as far away from Kym as possible. Last thing I need is for her to catch me all up in Claudia's grill.

"Freddie, I'm collecting hair for children with cancer. Holler at me if you cut your locks," she says, and I can't tell whether she's serious or not. She playfully cuts a strand of his hair with her fingers. Freddie nervously laughs. When we get into the hallway, she surprises me.

"You deserve a kiss, Omar." Really? It was that easy. I guess it was worth listening to Uncle Al, doing my little research online, almost making myself look like a fool at the rally. It's about to be on and popping.

"Once you feel these," I say, licking my lips, "you'll always be pleased."

"Then have two." Homegirl hands me two Hershey's chocolate Kisses. She laughs.

"That's cold."

"Looks like your plan worked, Omar Smalls. Your silent treatment was a success, it appears."

"That's what they're calling it: the silent treatment. That's what's up."

"Any teachers say anything to you?"

"Assistant Principal Walker stopped me in the hall after second period. I just told him it was a one-time senior prank. He told me Cruella's got her eye on me."

"I heard a few kids in ISS were talking, though." She stops at her locker.

"Some of the football players. I'll handle them jokers. One monkey don't stop the show." I look at her to see if she picks up on the reference. When I was in Brooklyn, my mom took me to see that play. It was boring, but I thought the title was a'ight. "It's a play, in case you was wondering."

"Wow. Omar Smalls didn't try to steal someone else's words."

"A lot you don't know about Omar Smalls," I say, moving her hair out of her face and behind her ear. Real playa move. I rest my hand on her shoulder. She shrugs it off. When she bends over to grab a book from the bottom of her locker, I can see her red panties. *Dayum!*

"So, what's next, T-Diddy?" she asks, still down there. I know exactly what's up.

"What's up is I want to make you dinner. Tonight."

"I'm talking about the protest, Omar. What's our next

step?" she asks, standing up and closing her locker. When she looks me in the eye, it's the first time I notice her stunning blue eyes. Or are they green? It's hard to tell in the barely lit hallway. The school board doesn't believe in lightbulbs either. Stunning. And homegirl has the best-smelling breath ever. Like peppermint. No doubt, we are having a moment.

It's time to pull out the big guns. None of T-Diddy's playa rules have worked, but a good quarterback always has a fail-safe plan. Mine is food. It's time to call an audible. Get homegirl to the crib and show her how T-Diddy gets down.

"I know what you meant, Claudia. It ain't over, believe that. Today was just the beginning."

"Your boy Belafonte has a plan. What's yours?" Dayum, she's serious about this arts funding ish. I love the band as much as everybody else, but why they sweating it so hard? It's the school board and the governor. They're not going to change ish because of our lame protest.

"It's only the first move, homegirl. We got some buzz. T-Diddy is in it to win it. Trust me on this, we're going to get all the arts funding back. Believe that." The smile on her face is priceless. She stands up and her eyes sparkle like diamonds. Definitely green.

It is a gamble, but I see checkmate three moves ahead. This is my chance. I go after her queen. I may drown, but I'm diving anyway.

"A'ight, forget about dinner. Let's come up with a plan tonight, my place, five thirty." I kiss her on the forehead and walk away. Your move, homegirl. Before I walk back inside the lunchroom, I want to turn around, to see if she's watching me. The playa's handbook says don't do it. But if I do and she is, then I know it's on.

"Omar," comes a yell from behind me. *Victory!*

Smiling, I happily turn around to see the principal standing not far from where Claudia was.

"We need to talk, Mr. Smalls."

Claudia

"Move your Jenny Craig rump, you're not the only one trying to look cute," Blu says, bumping me with her caboose so she can see herself in the mirror.

"My closet is bigger than your bathroom. Why we didn't use your mother's, I have no idea."

"I don't want her seeing these, that's why." Blu holds up her mother's MAC lipstick, paint stick, eye shadow, and Lustre Drops. I don't even know what Lustre Drops are, but it's MAC, so it is what it is.

"Oooh, I'm going to tell."

"And I'm going to tell Kym King you're going over to her dude's house."

"I changed my mind. I'm not going."

"Why am I not surprised?"

"I know what he's trying to do, so I'd be stupid to go over there. Unless you come with me."

"Girl, stop tripping. You saw all them kids he had at the rally. How many you think you woulda had? I'm just saying."

"I don't know."

"Uh, you're the one always talking about saving the world. Take one for the team. It's just a frickin' meeting, Claudia. Stop being a chump."

"Don't call me a chump."

"Then stop trippin' 'cause you find him attractive."

"What?"

"You know he looks good, girl."

"Whatever. Anyway, I'm not staying for more than thirty minutes."

"Girl, that's enough time for the candlelight dinner?"

"See, you got jokes."

"Well, all I have to say is, if I was into his fine football ass, which I'm obviously not, and he invited me over for dinner, the only plans being laid out would be me. I know that's right!" she says, cracking herself completely up.

"It's not dinner. He's a little cute, but too immature for me. Plus his reputation is horrible," I say.

"And? So is yours!" She laughs. She's right, but it's not the same. I get eyes rolled at me because I'm smart. And maybe a little snobbish. He's a ho and a cheater. That's a big difference. "Girl, he's slept with most of the cheerleaders and half the dance team, and they all talk about him like he's Tyrese or something. You better enjoy that meal tonight."

"Not going to happen, Blu. That's the problem with this school—everybody treats sex like it's not something big. Like you're not giving a piece of your soul to somebody."

"Is it that deep, Claudia? Really?"

"It is to me."

"Girl, why are you frontin' like you're a virgin? I know you let Leo hit, remember. Save that BS for school. Blu ain't no fool."

"Ugggh! Please don't say his name in here." Or I might puke. The drama that fool put me through is not what I want to be thinking about right now.

"Then don't try and play all bougie with me."

"I'm just saying. The guy has to mean something to me, to mean something to himself. He's got to take me there, ya know, before I let him take. Me. There." We high-five and laugh. Then I bump her so I can try some of those Lustre Drops before I head over to my "meeting."

"What's that smell?" I ask Omar, frowning.

"Oh, I just cooked up a little something."

"Omar, I told you I'd meet about the protest and that's it."

"Slow down, homegirl, why you always so tense? Chill for a minute."

"I'm outta here."

"Don't even act like it doesn't smell good. That's fresh food. Homemade. You should try it sometime."

No way. Mr. Football jerk has got this house smelling like tomato, basil, and garlic.

"Claudia, don't go. It was my night to make dinner. That's all. I'm almost done—then we can meet."

"Why does it say Library of Progress on the front door?" I ask him.

"During the day, my uncle runs a community service center here. Helping folks who need, uh, help." He takes my bag and motions for me to sit down on his couch. I choose a chair. "You look real good, Claudia."

"Whatever." He's wearing a muscle shirt, jeans, and apron with Miami's logo on the front. "Look, Omar, I hope you didn't really cook, because I can't stay for long. I've got an article to write for the paper tonight, and then Blu and I are rehearsing some routines for the dance team."

"Now who's playing who? It ain't no more dance team, homegirl. That's why we're meeting tonight. Chill—I'll be right back."

A few minutes later, he walks in with a plate that looks incredible, like it could be served in a restaurant.

"Don't worry, T-Diddy's not gonna keep you long. I got to get ready for my big press conference next week." He sets the tray down on the green-and-red table in front of me and leaves again. "Everybody wants to know which college T-Diddy chose."

It's obvious which college he's chosen. The banners on the wall, the ashtrays, his apron, the rug; they all make it pretty clear. I'm surprised he doesn't have a gold tooth with a big M on it.

"So you must be homegirl?" a bald-headed man with a long white beard says to me. I immediately stand up.

"Forgive my seat," he says to me with a slightly evil smile that reminds me of Omar's. Then he giggles and rolls his wheelchair over to the mozzarella and tomato Omar just brought in. "Sit down, little lady, get some of this antipasto. That mozzarella is fresh. The cow's name was Frankie." We both laugh.

He hands me a plate, and I sit back down on the couch. All of a sudden I feel a little stupid and unprepared. Why am I here? You loathe this guy, Claudia. And who is this old man in the wheelchair stuffing his face with cheese from a cow named Frankie?

"I see you've met Uncle Al," Omar says, placing another tray of food down on the table and removing what's left of the first. I can't even respond because of the piece of smoked mozzarella that's dancing inside my mouth. "I hope you enjoy the first course as much as you're enjoying that, Claudia." He smiles, sets a bowl of pasta with mushrooms and asparagus right in front of me, and walks back out. Am I being punked?

"Two things that boy knows how to do: throw a ball and make a meal. He's a genius," Uncle Al says. I finally finish chewing.

"I've never had cheese this good" is the only thing I can think to say.

"In the two years Smalls's been here, he's never cooked for a girl before. You must be something special," he says, scooping some pasta onto my plate.

"We're just working on some small stuff for school."

"A man makes a five-course meal for a woman, that's not some small stuff."

"*A five-course meal,*" I say, almost choking on a mushroom.

"You okay, Claudia? Smalls, bring the lady something to drink," Uncle Al yells into the kitchen. Omar comes out, in the middle of my very unattractive coughing. He hands me a wineglass with something red in it.

I've had wine twice in my life, not including communion on first Sundays at church. Once at Blu's bat mitzvah— her mother's Jewish—and once when I went to a college party with my ex. I hated it both times. But I was choking, I needed something.

"Don't worry, it's sparkling, nonalcoholic," Omar says. Who knew the jerk had another, more decent side? I drink the whole glass.

"Slow down, homegirl. We got like three more courses to go," Omar says, and then leaves for the third time. I'd be lying if I said I wasn't looking forward to what he came with next.

"So what's this thing y'all working on together?"

"Have you heard about the state arts funding cuts?"

"That's not the only thing your governor cut. Our funding got sliced, too. I might have to rob me a bank like them rappers to keep these doors open. I swear fo' Jesus, them politicians don't know nothing about nothing. Somebody needs to stand up to that madness."

"That's what we're working on, a protest. It started today."

"And Omar is helping you with that," he says, laughing.

"Yes, sir, it was actually his idea."

"That's interesting. I tried to get him to take a little petition next door and he tripped. Yeah, he likes you." I stuff a little more of the pasta in my mouth, hoping he gets the message that I really have nothing to say to that. "What are these, fritters?" I ask when Omar serves us the main course.

"This isn't store-bought shad, little lady. I caught this fish with my bare hands."

"Your bare hands, Uncle Al. Really," Omar says. "Claudia, we went fishing out at Folly. For the record, I cleaned it. With my bare hands."

Mr. Smalls says the grace, and I taste the first bite of fish. And the second. And twenty minutes later, after I've eaten three pieces of fish and I have to force myself not to ask for a fourth, all I can think is, WOW, this boy can cook!

Right before dessert, Uncle Al gets a phone call and excuses himself, leaving us alone. A little too convenient to be a coincidence.

OMG! Mocha chocolate cheesecake. It's better than good. He puts on the radio and it's the Slow Jamz hour. I just roll my eyes.

"What, I didn't know they were going to play that," he says. I kick off my shoes and almost put my feet on the couch . . . when he starts licking his lips, rocketing me back to reality.

"I didn't come here to have dinner with you, Omar. But yeah, thanks."

"I'm just glad you showed. Would have been wack if T-Diddy had cooked all them good eats and got stood up."

"It was really good. Where'd you learn how to cook like that?"

"T-Diddy can't tell his secrets."

"Seriously, enough with the T-Diddy this and T-Diddy that."

"When I was seven. I was at my cousin's house for Christmas, and she got a Betty Crocker oven. That joint was fire." I try not to laugh out loud but am unsuccessful. Mr. Football used to play with a Betty Crocker oven. Wow!

"Did you play with her Barbie also?" I laugh.

"Don't hate. I baked in that joint all day. Cried when I had to go home."

"Awwww!"

"My dad wouldn't buy me one, but my mom let me watch her cook dinner every night. I've been cooking ever since. Only reason I started playing ball was because my dad wanted to toughen me up."

"So you don't even like football?"

"I love football. I just love cooking, too. It's sorta like if you had kids, could you love one more than the other? Not possible."

"If you were one of the kids, then yeah, very possible," I say, and playfully jab him in the stomach. His abs are rock hard. "Nice, uh, shirt." Oh my!

"Look, no flirting. This is not a date. We're meeting, remember?" he says, catching me off guard. I punch him in his arm. That's twice I've touched him in five seconds. I'm feeling some kind of way. He throws his arm over the couch behind me. When did he get this close? I slide back a little. His arms are trees.

"So what's the plan, Mr. Football?" I ask, inching away a little more. You're not slick, Omar.

"Simple. We keep it up. Every day we add five minutes to the protest. Eventually they're going to decide to do the right thing."

"What if they don't? What if it goes on for like weeks?"

"All that is good and accomplished in this world takes work."

"Who said that?"

"Me. Just now." I smirk at him. "I don't know, I read it somewhere."

If it wasn't for the piece of basil lodged in his front teeth, the awkward moment might get the best of me. I should tell him. Not.

"Look, I tweeted it right before you got here. And I posted it on Facebook. It's on for tomorrow, Claudia. You would have known that if you'd accepted my friend request."

"I think we should give the principal our demands."

"Ya think?"

"We should give her a list of things we expect her and the school board to do. Jobs reinstated. Arts funding restored, all that."

"You think that will work?"

"I don't know, but eventually they are going to ask us to stop the silent protest, and we're going to tell them we will, but only if—"

"They meet our demands. Right! That's what's up, Claudia Clarke. You're a pro at this revolution stuff."

Why is it so hot in here?

"What's the end goal?" I ask him, sweat tickling under my arms. "Are we going to be able to save the teachers' jobs?" He puts his left leg on the couch. It brushes mine.

"We've got to get the arts funding back. Why is it so hot in here?" He wipes my forehead. "Will this really do anything?" I'm talking so much, so many questions, I don't even see him until he's inches away from me. My hair drapes his chest. I can smell the sweat on his head. His mustache tickles the air between us. And then it happens.

He takes a finger and softly slides my hair from my face, and around my neck, just like he did at my locker. He does this two times, not saying anything. The basil is still there, but it's not funny anymore. I can't move. Did he give me one of those date-rape drugs? Seriously, I'm paralyzed. Now he moves his fingers up to my bottom lip and rubs it slowly. Then he kisses me. Or tries to. Right before the front door opens.

"Good thing I forgot my wallet." In the second it takes me to turn my head and see Omar's uncle roll in the front door, Omar defies time and space and circumstance. He sneaks a kiss. It happens so fast. It is soft and hard and now my heart is about to jump out of my chest. Or the palm of my hand is about to collide with his face.

"Uh-oh, Al, they got on Usher. That there is baby-making music," I hear someone say.

Embarrassment doesn't even begin to describe how I feel.

"I have to get home," I say, grabbing my jacket and sprinting for the door.

"You ain't gotta leave on account of Spooky. He was just messin'."

"Hole up, hole up! Claudia, wait," I hear Omar say, but I ignore him.

I'm five minutes away when I realize I'm not wearing any shoes.

OMAR

Tdiddy Smalls Fifteen minutes at silent protest 2morrow.
Happy birthday, Dr. King #SpeakUpNow
Unlike · Comment · Share · @DaRealTDiddy · Wednesday at
5:00 pm ·
👍 **You, Freddie Callaway, Blu McCants, Savannah Gadsden**
and 39 others like this.

> View 26 more comments
> **Luther Lee** Hey, Omar, you're a cool dude. Count me in.
> Wednesday at 5:05 pm via mobile · Like
>
> **Eve Chappell** I AM VERY PROUD OF U!!!
> Wednesday at 5:05 pm · Like
>
> **Andy Washington** No justice, no peace! I'm down with
> the cause.
> Wednesday at 5:21 pm · Like

Savannah Gadsden ☺
Wednesday at 5:21 pm · Like

Freddie Callaway Savannah, that's Mr. Washington, the government teacher. Bwahahahahahaha!
Wednesday at 5:23 pm · Like

Savannah Gadsden Really? ROFLAICGU!
Wednesday at 5:24 pm · Like

Kym King And to think . . . I almost believed him this time around.
Wednesday at 9:10 pm · Like

Kym King ☹
Wednesday at 9:55 pm via Mobile · Like

Tdiddy Smalls My bad. I had a meeting.
Wednesday at 10:40 pm · Like

Freddie Calloway Bong bong?
Wednesday at 11:31 pm · Unlike · 👍 **You** like this.

Freddie Callaway Dawg, you see Mr. Washington on your page. Creepy.
Wednesday at 11:35 pm · Like

Andy Washington Hey, Freddie.
Wednesday at 11:36 pm · Like

Freddie Callaway Bwahahahahahaha!
Wednesday at 11:36 pm · Like

Andy Washington Hey, what does ROFLAICGU mean?
Wednesday at 11:37 pm · Like

Tdiddy Smalls What up, Mr. Washington. No offense,
but how you get up here?
Wednesday at 11:37 pm · Like

Andy Washington I sent you a friend request and you
accepted. I'm number 4751. You got a lot of friends, Omar.
Wednesday at 11:38 pm · Like

Tdiddy Smalls *Rolling on the floor laughing and I can't
get up*
Wednesday at 11:40 pm · Like

Andy Washington Oh, I get it. Ha ha! Just trying to
stay hip, Omar. Gotta go. Bong bong!
Wednesday at 11:40 pm · Like

Blu McCants Let me find out you can cook.
Wednesday at 11:40 pm · Unlike · 👍 **You** like this.

Freddie Callaway *Trying to stay hip*
Bwahahahahaha! *
Wednesday at 11:41 pm · Like

Tdiddy Smalls Freddie, did that woadie just say *bong bong* LOLOL!
Wednesday at 11:41 pm · Like

Tdiddy Smalls Got to risk it to get the biscuit.
Wednesday at 11:42 pm via mobile · Like

Blu McCants For real though, thanks for doing this with my girl. #silent treatment.
Wednesday at 11:46 pm · Like

Andy Washington What is a woadie?
Thursday at 1:36 am · Like

Playbeezy Carolina Hood Woadie ▶ Tdiddy Smalls
Everybody go check out the new single "We Stealin' Yo Babies" Feat. <u>Ricky Rozay</u> and <u>Hoe Daddy</u> by <u>PlayBeezy</u>. Free downloads available as well. . . . Go listen to it, support the CHUCKTOWN movement.
Unlike · Comment · Share · Thursday at 3:26 am ·
👍 **You, Willie Mack, Tami Hill** and 4 others like this.

Freddie Callaway Go to sleep nucka!
Thursday at 3:34 am via mobile · Like

Tdiddy Smalls Bwahahahahahahaha!

Thursday at 3:34 am · Like

Belafonte Jones ▶ **Tdiddy Smalls** Who's riding with the Marching Panthers?

Unlike · Comment · Share · Thursday at 7:31 am ·

👍 **You** like this.

    Belafonte Jones Save the band!

    Thursday at 7:33 am · Like

    Tdiddy Smalls Ride.

    Thursday at 7:34 am · Like

    Tami Hill Ride.

    Thursday at 7:34 am · Like

    Eve Chappell Ride.

    Thursday at 7:36 am · Like

    Leah Rivers Ride.

    Thursday at 7:37 am · Like

    Freddie Callaway Ride.

    Thursday at 7:37 am · Like

    Blu McCants Ride.

    Thursday at 7:38 am · Like

Tdiddy Smalls Shhhhhhhhhhhhh! #SpeakUpNow

Unlike · Comment · Share · @DaRealTDiddy · Thursday at 8:14 am ·

👍 109 people like this.

Belafonte Jones Thanks to everyone who supported the silent protest, includingthe teachers who rode with us!

Unlike · Comment · Share · Thursday at 11:31 am via mobile ·

👍 **You** and 73 people like this.

Tdiddy Smalls We did the damn thing today. Martin Luther King would be proud of WCHS today! We back on that joint tomorrow! Heading to the gym to get my lift on. #SpeakUpNow

Unlike · Comment · Share · @DaRealTDiddy · Thursday at 5:40 pm ·

👍 **You**, **Andy Washington**, **Leah Rivers** and 177 others like this.

View 55 more comments

Luther Lee Power to the people.

Thursday at 5:51 pm via mobile · Like

Tdiddy Smalls The party just started, homeboy.

Thursday at 5:51 pm · Like

Sami Schmidt Mr. Smalls, I'm the president of the Deep Creek SGA and we heard about the protest. We want to do the same.

Thursday at 5:52 pm · Like

Luther Lee We fired up. . . .
Thursday at 5:52 pm via mobile · Like

Belafonte Jones We ain't takin' no mo'!!!!!!!
Thursday at 5:52 pm · Like

Tami Hill I miss the band.
Thursday at 5:52 pm · Like

Blu McCants True.
Thursday at 5:52 pm · Like

Freddie Callaway I did the math. We keep dis up
for like three weeks, and ain't nobody saying ish all
day.
Thursday at 5:53 pm via mobile · Like

Tdiddy Smalls Me and Claudia don't think it's going to
take three weeks.
Thursday at 5:54 pm · Like

Leah Rivers Take three weeks for what?
Thursday at 5:54 pm via mobile · Like

Tdiddy Smalls For us to get what we want. We have a
list of demands.
Thursday at 5:54 pm · Like

Freddie Callaway I hope you got cookies and cream on that list.
Thursday at 5:54 pm via mobile · Like

Tdiddy Smalls **SMH**
Thursday at 5:54 pm · Like

Sami Schmidt Mr. Smalls, our funding got cut for the arts too. Our drama department is one of the best in the state and now we no longer have it. Everybody is pissed.
Thursday at 5:55 pm · Like

Willie Mack *Mr. Smalls* As if his head ain't big enough.
Thursday at 5:55 pm · Like

Tdiddy Smalls That's what's up, Sami. I'll let Claudia know.
Thursday at 5:56 pm · Like

Kym King That's why you ain't come over? That Claudia Clarke trick.
Thursday at 5:57 pm · Like

Kym King Sooo beyond irritated at this point . . . I shoulda known she was scheming at that party . . . stuck-up trick . . . her and her butch best friend.
Thursday at 5:57 pm · Like

Freddie Callaway WOW!

Thursday at 5:57 pm · Like

Blu McCants Females wonder why I give them absolutely NO respect. . . . It's about time I step out of character at West Charleston. . . . That will put an end to all this nonsensical drama. . . . **cocking my chamber**

Thursday at 5:57 pm · Like

Tdiddy Smalls @Kym why you trippin'. That's foul! You just played yourself.

Thursday at 5:59 pm · Like

Blu McCants Omar, you betta check your girl.

Thursday at 5:59 pm · Like

Blu McCants I can't deal with these insecure females. . . . Only in the country is this acceptable.

Thursday at 5:59 pm · Like

Willie Mack What happened to "We Shall Overcome"?

Thursday at 5:59 pm · Like

Freddie Callaway Ol' girl went sideways.

Thursday at 5:59 pm · Like

Tdiddy Smalls Sorry 'bout that y'all.

Thursday at 5:59 pm · Like

Fredro Parcel, Jr. Omar, this Fredro from the U. We met on your recruiting weekend. Yo, your FB joints be funny as hell. How are your off-season workouts going?
Thursday at 6:13 pm via mobile · Like

Tdiddy Smalls Two hundred sit-ups. Now I'm gonna eat, take a shower. Who wanna tuck Tdiddy in tonight?
Thursday at 9:40 pm · Like

Tami Hill What time?
Thursday at 9:55 pm via mobile · Like

Tdiddy Smalls Hate to sound sleazy, but tease me, I don't want it if it's that easy. . . .
Thursday at 10:06 pm · Like

Rich Smalls YOU TRIP ME OUT w/ all yo dumb statuses and how you have so many girls after you . . . lol
Thursday at 10:11 pm · Like

Tdiddy Smalls What up, cuz!
Thursday at 10:11 pm · Like

Rich Smalls Playa
Thursday at 10:12 pm via mobile · Like

Tdiddy Smalls You holding down BK. I miss the Apple, fo' sho.
Thursday at 10:12 pm · Like

116

Rich Smalls Look like you holdin' it down in Charleston.
Thursday at 10:12 pm via mobile · Like

Tdiddy Smalls You know how we do. You living large, homeboy?
Thursday at 10:12 pm · Like

Rich Smalls Son, I make it do what it do. Pushing that Tahoe.
Thursday at 10:13 pm via mobile · Like

Tdiddy Smalls Your mom's. LOL!
Thursday at 10:14 pm · Like

Rich Smalls Don't sleep, Omar. I do my thing.
Thursday at 10:14 pm via mobile · Like

Tdiddy Smalls That's whas up! I'm coming home for spring break.
Thursday at 10:15 pm · Like

Rich Smalls I'll holla. My break's over and somebody just came thru the drive-thru.
Thursday at 10:15 pm via mobile · Like

Tdiddy Smalls is now friends with **Claudia Clarke** and 11 other people.

You poked **Claudia Clarke**.

Tdiddy Smalls ▶ Claudia Clarke Thanks for the add, homegirl!
Like · Comment · Share · Thursday at 11:01 pm

Tdiddy Smalls ▶ Freddie Callaway I unfriended Kym and Mr. Washington. LOL!
Like · Comment · Share · Thursday at 11:07 pm

Chat started Thursday, January 17

Claudia Clarke Stop poking me.

Tdiddy Smalls Return my call then.

Claudia Clarke Been busy

Tdiddy Smalls I looked for you at lunch today.

Tdiddy Smalls Your feet cold?

Claudia Clarke Whatever.

Tdiddy Smalls It's all good! You have a good time?

Claudia Clarke Please don't say anything to anybody about what happened.

Tdiddy Smalls What happened?

Claudia Clarke Don't play dumb. You tried to kiss me.

Tdiddy Smalls Actually, homegirl, I did kiss you. How was it for you?

Claudia Clarke It doesn't even matter.

Tdiddy Smalls Exactly!

Tdiddy Smalls You still there?

Claudia Clarke Whatever! I'm here.

Tdiddy Smalls The protest was pretty tight, right? Even some of the teachers joined in. That's what's up!

Claudia Clarke My guidance counselor said the principal was pissed. She asked me was I involved. I told her not really.

Tdiddy Smalls You punked out? Cru scared you, homegirl.

Tdiddy Smalls S . . . L . . . O . . . W . . . T . . . Y . . . P . . . A

Tdiddy Smalls ZzzzzzzzzzzzzzzzzzzzzzzzzZZZZ

Claudia Clarke She just said I needed to be careful, because Harvard might rescind my acceptance if I have some negative conduct-type stuff on my transcript.

Tdiddy Smalls Yeah, my coach said the same thing, but no way Miami's passing up on T-Diddy Smalls. Believe that! That's cool you going to Harvard.

Claudia Clarke I know.

Tdiddy Smalls SMH . . . twenty minutes tomorrow. You ready?

Claudia Clarke I'm ready, are you?

Tdiddy Smalls T-Diddy can't stop, won't stop. Believe that!

Claudia Clarke Thanks for dinner. I gotta go.

Tdiddy Smalls Let's get together again . . .

Tdiddy Smalls I really did enjoy that kiss. I could learn to love those lush lips, homegirl.

Tdiddy Smalls Come to the party with me tomorrow night.

Claudia Clarke Good-bye.

Tdiddy Smalls Yeah, I heard you the first time you said it. So you're gonna act like that kiss didn't mean anything?

Claudia Clarke It wasn't a kiss, Omar. I'm not going to be another one-hit wonder for you. I'm looking for a guy who wants to change the world, not win a game. Let's stick to the protest please.

Tdiddy Smalls Can we at least get together one evening? I could really use some help with my senior paper. As friends, of course.

Claudia Clarke Maybe next week, GTG! Oh, bring my shoes to school tomorrow. Please.

* * *

Freddie Calloway Shhhhhhhhhhhh—with Tdiddy Smalls.
Twenty minutes!
Unlike · Comment · Share · Friday at 8:14 am ·
👍 **You** and 64 others like this.

Tdiddy Smalls at the house party on Dorchester.
Where my dawgs at!!!!
Like · Comment · Share · Friday at 10:04 pm ·
👍 **Willie Mack**, **Freddie Callaway** and 19 others like this.

> **Freddie Callaway** On my way! Gotta drop my sista at
> the movies.
> Friday at 10:10 pm via mobile · Like

> **Eve Chappell** I'M SO DRUNK RAT NOW
> Friday at 10:14 pm · Like

> **Belafonte Jones** I heard them Bayside boys comin'
> thru. I got your back!
> Friday at 10:16 pm via mobile · Like

> **Tami Hill** Eve, where you at?
> Friday at 10:17 pm · Like

Willie Mack ▶ Tdiddy Smalls Them jokers was tryin' to
fight us for real.
Like · Comment · Share · Saturday at 12:04 am ·

View 43 more comments

Tdiddy Smalls I ain't kno D had a jammy jam. Them boys got ghost quick.
Saturday at 12:08 am via mobile · Like

Blu McCants Y'all need to stop all that craziness fore somebody get hurt.
Saturday at 12:08 am · Like

Willie Mack Stop trippin, Blu. They the ones comin' up here starting ish.
Saturday at 12:08 am via mobile · Like

Johnny "Moose" Dawkins And we gonna be the ones to finish that shit too!
Saturday at 12:09 am · Like

Freddie Callaway I know this nucka not on your page, T.
Saturday at 12:09 am via mobile · Like

Johnny "Moose" Dawkins You ought to be careful who you friend, Titty. Tornados comin' after that ass.
Saturday at 12:09 am · Like

Tdiddy Smalls C'mon son! We already beat y'all once. Ain't no thing to do it again.
Saturday at 12:10 am via mobile · Like

Savannah Gadsden Y'all needs to chill!

Saturday at 12:11 am · Like

Johnny "Moose" Dawkins Watch your back! Your punk boy ain't have no heater, we woulda dropped them Bayside B's on y'all!

Saturday at 12:12 am · Like

Tdiddy Smalls Get off my page!

Saturday at 12:12 am via mobile · Like

Ambiene Lewis Go Tornados! I'm riding Bayside till I die.

Saturday at 12:12 am · Like

Tdiddy Smalls blocked

Saturday at 12:13 am via mobile · Like

Eve Chappell T-Diddy, invest in some hand sanitizer so when the hataz shake ya hand . . .

Saturday at 12:14 am · Like

Freddie Callaway Tami, don't give Eve no more hooch.

Saturday at 12:14 am via mobile · Like

Tdiddy Smalls Score! #Leggo #Jets

Like · Comment · Share · @DaRealTdiddy · Sunday at 3:04 pm ·

You poked **Claudia Clarke**.

Tdiddy Smalls Claudia Clarke "At the center of nonviolence stands the principle of love." #MLKHoliday
Like · Comment · Share · @DaRealTdiddy · Monday at 10:20 am ·
👍 **You**, **Claudia Clarke**, **Blu McCants** and 212 others like this.

> View 95 more comments
> **Freddie Callaway** No school today. T-Diddy, you cooking?
> Monday at 10:22 am · Like
>
> **Savannah Gadsden** "A man who won't die for something is not fit to live." (MLK)
> Monday at 10:23 am · Like
>
> **Claudia Clarke** "An individual has not started living until he can rise above the narrow confines of his individualistic concerns to the broader concerns of all humanity."
> Monday at 10:26 am · Like
>
> **Tdiddy Smalls** "Freedom is never voluntarily given by the oppressor; it must be demanded by the oppressed."
> Monday at 10:26 am · Like
>
> **Belafonte Jones** "Beautiful music is the art of the prophets that can calm the agitations of the soul; it is one of the most magnificent and delightful presents God has given us."
> Monday at 10:26 am · Like

Tami Hill "I look to a day when people will not be judged by the color of their skin, but by the content of their character."
Monday at 10:27 am · Like

Freddie Callaway "A man can't ride your back unless it's bent." Bwahahahahaha!
Monday at 10:27 am · Like

Tdiddy Smalls C'mon son.
Monday at 10:27 am · Like

Freddie Callaway What??!! He said that joint, T-Diddy!
Monday at 10:27 am · Like

Blu McCants "A riot is the language of the unheard."
Monday at 10:28 am · Like

Luther Lee "The time is always right to do what is right."
Monday at 10:30 am · Like

Eve Chappell I can't help but notice that awesome ends in ME and ugly starts with U.
Monday at 10:35 am · Like

Freddie Callaway ROFLMAO!!!!!!
Monday at 10:36 am · Like

Luther Lee "We must all learn to live together as

brothers or perish together as fools."
Monday at 10:36 am · Like

Willie Mack Why y'all fools awake? It's a holiday. Go
the F@#& back to sleep! ZZZZZZzzzzzzzzzzzzzz . . .
Monday at 10:51 am · Like

Blu McCants **SMH**
Monday at 10:51 am · Like

Tdiddy Smalls Shhhhhhhhhhhhh! DAY FIVE!!!!!!!!
#SpeakUpNow
Unlike · Comment · Share · @DaRealTdiddy · Tuesday at 8:15 am ·
👍 **You**, **Claudia Clarke**, **Freddie Callaway** and 233 others like this.

Freddie Callaway Dawg, we gotta be quiet for thirty
minutes. That's hard as hell. #ijs
Tuesday at 8:15 am via mobile · Like

Tdiddy Smalls Claudia Clarke, will you go to the ball with me?
Unlike · Comment · Share · Tuesday at 9:00 pm via mobile
👍 **You**, **Claudia Clarke**, **Freddie Callaway** and 19 others like this.

Claudia Clarke Really, Omar?
Tuesday at 9:45 pm via mobile · Like

Tdiddy Smalls Yeah, I figured since I already know the
shoe fits, we can keep it movin' #cinderella
Tuesday at 9:45 pm via mobile · Like

Claudia Clarke ROFL!
Tuesday at 9:48 pm via mobile · Like

Blu McCants Awwwwwww? My bestie's going to the prom.
Tuesday at 9:49 pm via mobile · Like

Claudia Clarke I'm not going to the prom with anybody, and if I was, the dude wouldn't have asked me to go on the Facebooks.
Tuesday at 9:50 pm via mobile · Like

Tami Hill I'll go.
Tuesday at 9:51 pm via mobile · Like

Blu McCants Only in the country . . .
Tuesday at 9:52 pm via mobile · Like

Tdiddy Smalls Baller Alert: Tomorrow's a BIG DAY! T-Diddy is on the radio tomorrow morning at six a.m. . . . T-Diddy press conference tomorrow after school in the gym. Holla at yo' boy!
Like · Comment · Share · Tuesday at 10:06 pm ·

Luther Lee TURN ON POWER 103 JAMZ Tdiddy Smalls
Like · Comment · Share · Wednesday at 6:15 am via mobile
⚐ **Claudia Clarke, Freddie Callaway, Luther Lee** and 18 others like this.

Eve Chappell Tdiddy's on the morning show. You sound good.
Wednesday at 6:15 am via mobile · Like

Freddie Callaway That woadie talking about Miami?
Wednesday at 6:15 am via mobile · Like

Eve Chappell Naw! They talking about the silent protest. The mayor's on there now.
Wednesday at 6:15 am via mobile · Like

Blu McCants Thirty-five minutes today #shhhhh
Wednesday at 6:16 am via mobile · Like

Tami Hill What channel? I can't see him.
Wednesday at 6:16 am via mobile · Like

Freddie Callaway **SMFH!!!!!!** **
Wednesday at 6:17 am via mobile · Like

Willie Mack "If you don't stand for something, you'll fall for anything." —T-Diddy
Wednesday at 6:18 am via mobile · Like

Tdiddy Smalls Shhhhhhhhhhh!
Wednesday at 6:19 am via mobile · Like

Freddie Callaway Bwahahahahaha!
Wednesday at 6:20 am via mobile · Like

Blu McCants Claudia said call her.
Wednesday at 6:21 am via mobile · Like

Willie Mack Uh-oh!
Wednesday at 6:21 am via mobile · Like

Tdiddy Smalls Ha ha! It's all good.
Wednesday at 6:21 am via mobile · Like

Dr. Brenda Jackson Actually, it isn't. Come see me
first thing this morning, Mr. Smalls. And bring Ms. Clarke
with you.
Wednesday at 6:24 am via mobile · Like

Claudia

"I understand, believe me. When I was at Spelman, we protested every other weekend. What you've both done is good. It's good for our school; for the students, whether they know it or not. It keeps our elected officials honest. The truth is, I don't want to lose the arts funding any more than you do, but my hands are tied. Something had to be cut. We must find a way to make do under the current economic struggles. We must tighten the belt a little," Dr. Jackson says, like she's running for office or something. I instantly feel like she's patronizing us, and I so want to tell her to cut the BS.

"With all due respect, Dr. J. , save the BS. The funding for the new football stadium wasn't cut," Omar says confidently and defiantly. It doesn't even come out disrespectfully; more like he's a journalist. The fire in his voice is measured. And kinda sexy as hell.

"Mr. Smalls, let's not forget who's the student and who's the adult here," a shocked Dr. Jackson says.

"These are our demands," I say, and hand her our list. She laughs, but I ignore that and continue. "As you can see, there are only five, so we'd appreciate your prompt attention to this matter."

"This silent mess ends now, you two understand?" she shouts. Her smile is gone, replaced by an irritated frown. "I've gotten calls from two other principals, and it seems that your little prank has spread to two other schools. It ends now."

"This is not a prank, Dr. Jack—"

"I'm still talking, Mr. Smalls," she says, her face all scrunched up.

"Claudia, I'm surprised at you. Number one in your class, Harvard bound, most likely to succeed. This is what you want your legacy to be? Don't forget, I wrote you that recommendation, and I can just as easily send them a revision." Now she's just being spiteful, as evidenced by the vein popping out of her forehead.

"Dr. Jackson, here's the thing, we—"

"I'm speaking, Mr. Smalls. With all the trouble the Miami athletic department is in, how do you think they are going to take you being suspended, or worse, expelled from school?"

Now she's standing up, pointing her finger at us. I never even thought about what kind of impact our protest is having on her. And her job security.

I'm sure she heard Omar on the radio. Just like the mayor and the school board. And I'm sure her boss, the superintendent, and his boss, the frickin' school board, told her to fix it. It's sad that she's got caught in the middle, but the truth is we couldn't stop this protest if we wanted to. We don't. The students are too amped up. They want band, gospel choir, drama, and art back. And they . . . we . . . are going to be quiet until we get it.

"Teachers should be happy we aren't all loud in class like we normally are," Omar says to her, which really fumes her up.

"That's the problem. You don't even see the consequences of your actions. Life has been real good, for both of you. But I tell you what, if you don't end this protest immediately . . ." And she doesn't finish her sentence, she just picks up her phone and dials a number.

I'm wondering if she's calling our homes, or the police. Finally she talks into the phone.

"Coach, yes. This is Dr. Jackson. That big press conference you scheduled for later today? Yes, the one for Omar Smalls to make his college announcement. Well, it's canceled. Yes, I know. Hold on one minute." She looks up at Omar, smiles, and says, "Consequences, Mr. Smalls, there are always consequences. And, Ms. Clarke, try me if you want, but don't think I can't shut down the *Panther Pride* website. You two can go now."

Silent Treatment

by Claudia Clarke

Recently, on 103 Jamz, Omar "T-Diddy" Smalls told Deja Dee, the morning show host, "If you don't stand for something, you will fall for anything." The students at West Charleston High School have finally decided to stand up for themselves, and for what they believe in. A little over a week ago, almost eight hundred students rallied on a Thursday morning to protest arts funding cuts. Students packed the sidewalks and lawn around the high school in a show of support for teachers and the various arts programs that were affected as the city has grappled with cutting its budget. At the rally, Mr. Smalls tasked each student with remaining quiet during the first ten minutes of homeroom, in a show of solidarity.

"It has been an extremely peaceful and creative demonstration," government teacher Mr. Washington said of the protest, which has now gone on for seven days.

"The administration is not pleased at what we're doing. They're even making threats against some students. But we will not stand by and let them destroy the very heart and soul of education: the arts," an anonymous student texted.

"It's hard to tell whether it will work," Mr. Washington added, "but it's definitely important for students to feel empowered." When asked if the protest will continue, Smalls said check his Facebook page. Click here to visit Omar Smalls's Facebook page.

Students Go Apes

by Blu McCants

In October, a group of students organized a movie night fundraiser to raise money for Save the Chimps, a Florida-based nonprofit that offers permanent care to rescued chimpanzees. The local West Charleston Movie Theater showed a special 3D screening of *Rise of the Planet of the Apes* and donated all proceeds from ticket sales and popcorn to the fundraising effort. Bananas were also given out to each moviegoer, courtesy of the Awendaw Farmers' market. "We raised over five hundred dollars, which will go toward housing the more than three hundred chimpanzees who were rescued from a lab in Texas," said Luther Lee, a coorganizer along with Claudia Clarke. "The animals were living in horrible conditions, and now they're in heaven." Not literally, of course. More fundraisers are being planned, as Save the Chimps is hoping to raise $10,000 to rescue more chimpanzees.

The "A" Word

by Claudia Clarke

Abortions in South Carolina rose 10 percent last year. According to a local study, the data shows higher rates of births and abortions among girls fifteen to nineteen. We've already talked about the staggering teen pregnancy numbers at our school, but this stat is outrageous, people. If we are to be productive women in this society, we must become better educated about abstinence and ways to avoid pregnancy in the first place. Whether you are pro-choice or pro-life, it doesn't matter. What matters is that we treat ourselves with respect. What matters is that we take our bodies seriously. Many girls use abortion as a form of birth control. That is ignorant and irresponsible. We have to do better, people. For more info on this matter, visit <u>Planned Parenthood</u>.

"You can't get a dude, so you gotta steal mine." I'm in the front yard waiting for Blu, minding my own business, when they come up.

"Kym, I don't know what you're talking about," I answer, and wish I hadn't told Blu I'd come to the house party with her.

"Come on now, Claudia, don't get all scared now. You all up on his Facebook page and whatnot," Eve adds, egging her on.

"He didn't even get to do his big press thing 'cause of you," Kym says. "It was his big day, and you ruined that for him."

"How did I ruin it?"

"'Cause you triflin'." Eve laughs. "I'm only gonna say this once. Stay away from Kym's man, trick."

Where is Blu? These girls want to fight.

"Hole up, hole up, I know you ain't talking about me, Kym," Omar says, with a beer in his hand. Not that I needed him to come to my rescue. Kym is silent now, like the people in the front yard watching us. "Pay attention, everybody!" he yells at the top of his lungs, and everybody stops and looks at us. People from inside the house start filing out into the yard. "Breaking news, people. T-Diddy and Kym King are no longer together. We broke up two weeks ago. Real talk!"

"Who you dating now?" somebody screams. T-Diddy, Kym, and Eve all look at me, and I want to be as far away from this nonsense as possible. So I go inside.

"Wait up, Claudia," I hear Omar say, and by the time I get to the front door, he's holding it open for me.

"What was that all about?" he asks.

"Like I should know," I say, and roll my eyes. "It's too crowded in here. Jeez." I make my way over to a closed door, to get away from all the chaos while I wait for Blu.

When we get to the door, it opens, and Fast Freddie and Belafonte trail a hurricane of smoke.

"I don't think you want to go in the hot box, homegirl," Omar says, and pulls me away. "Let's go out back and talk."

"Here, take this," I say, and hand him a mint.

"It's just beer," he says.

"It just stinks." He pops the mint in his mouth. "Sorry about your press conference, Omar."

"I ain't bitter. It's no big deal," he says, trying to sound like it doesn't faze him, but I can hear it in his voice.

"I know how important it was to you."

"You want to make it up to me?" he asks with that evil grin he makes where one eyebrow rises. "Come with me to Folly."

"Never give up, huh?"

"Seriously, let's go for a walk on the beach. I need to clear my mind."

"It's not your mind I'm worried about."

"I got a plan on how we can step up our game on this silent treatment."

"How?"

"You'll see," he says, and part of me thinks he has no idea, but the other part of me can't wait to see what he comes up with this time. "Let's give these jokers one more week to do the right thing, and if they don't, we'll get three-six-mafia up in here."

"Huh?"

"Start a riot." I give him a look that says "You're crazy." "I was speaking metaphorically, Claudia."

"What about Cru?"

"C'mon. She was trying to play us. I called the coach at Miami, and he said as long as I don't kill nobody or end up in jail, my scholarship is good as gold."

"Wow! You're really serious about this."

"When T-Diddy gets an idea in his head, he can't let go. Gotta run with it till he scores. Feel me."

"It's too chilly to be walking on the beach."

"It's sixty-one degrees." He shows me the temperature on his iPhone. "Come on, be spontaneous, homegirl."

"Let's dance, Mr. Football." This is about as spontaneous as you're going to get from me.

He grabs my hand, and we walk back inside to the dance floor. He can't dance that well, but he's tall, so all he really has to do is stand over me and wave his hands from side to side, which he does pretty well. The next song that comes on is a slow song, and he just looks at me. I see Kym and Eve eyeing me from the corner. Now what, heifers? If I wanted your man, I could have him.

I put my arms up around his neck. He slides his around my waist and then moves them to the pockets of my jeans. I move them back up to my waist. I see Kym gritting on me, so I pull him closer.

OMAR

I never let a broad play me out of position. Got to stay focused on the mission at hand. Focus, focus, focus.

Ever since the protest started, I haven't worked out as much. Haven't hung out with Willie Mack and Fast Freddie as much. I even missed the third quarter of the Jets game last Sunday to talk on the phone with Claudia. What's up with that?

I'm minutes from closing the deal with homegirl, I can feel it, but the truth is, I'm starting to feel a certain kinda way when I'm around her. Don't get me wrong, it's not like I want her for my wifey. But I can see keeping her around for a while. Maybe. Don't forget why you came here, homeboy. T-Diddy, snap out of this. Dive in her ocean and get out, playa.

Tonight may be the night. I need to lock this up now. I inch my hands down to her jeans and cup her cheeks. She pushes them back up. Still playing hard to get. Wait, she pulls me closer to her, grinds a little. Homegirl got me vexed. I don't know if she wants T-Diddy or not.

I see Willie Mack and Fast Freddie on the dance floor getting their freak on with some sophomores. They're basically doing it right there. Time for me step up my game, for real.

I move my hands back down, but this time, I go inside her jeans. Now that's what I'm talking about. This is all me, homegirl.

"What are you doing, Omar?" She pushes me away from her.

"Why you screamin', Claudia? I'm sorry. I didn't mean to—"

"Are you drunk?" Every nosy character in West Charleston is all up in our convo now. Claudia is loud as heck. The music stops, and it seems like the whole party is watching us. T-Diddy can't have no broad disrespecting him like that.

"Naw, girl, ain't nobody drunk."

"So why are you tripping?"

"Didn't *you* pull me on the dance floor?"

"Yeah! To dance."

"What, you ain't like T-Diddy's moves?" My boys and several other party people laugh, and I laugh it up with them. "Lighten up, homegirl, you killing the buzz. Hey, DJ, turn the music back up. Ain't no party like a Panther party, 'cause a Panther party don't stop."

The lights go back down, the music blasts, the party resumes, and Claudia storms out the front door. I chase her, but Kym steps in my way.

"Omar, you're too good for that skank. Let her go, keep it moving. I ain't gonna keep waiting on you."

"Then don't. Now, step."

"Karma is a bitch, Omar. Watch your back," she says, and flicks her wrist at me like she's casting a spell or something.

Outside, I see Claudia half a block away, getting into her car, about to be ghost. I sprint and jump in front of her car, so she can't, at least not without running me over.

"Can we talk, please?"

"Out of my way, Omar. I swear!"

"T-Diddy ain't moving. Get out and talk to me."

"You really know how to be a jerk, don't you?" She jumps out of her car.

"Thank you. Look, Claudia, I'm sorry."

"Don't be. You showed your true colors, primate."

"What about the kiss?"

"There was no kiss. You're delusional."

"I know your tongue moved."

"I wasn't myself."

"What, you an alien or something?"

"It was a mistake. A minor lapse in my judgment. I should have followed my first instinct and slapped you silly."

"That kiss, your lips, this thing we have is not minor. It's major."

"Sounds like a song I've heard on the radio."

"No comment."

"Stop trying to play me. Look, you got your kiss, you copped a feel. Ain't that enough to claim your prize? Leave me the frick alone."

"The frick? WOW!" I say, laughing. "Claudia, will you forgive me for tonight?"

"Look, Omar, we're friends, that's all. Actually, we're not even that."

"I thought we had a thing. We were feeling each other."

"A thing? You don't even know me?"

"I do know you, girl."

"What's my favorite color?"

"Red."

"Green! What's my favorite flower?"

"Rose."

"Tulip. This is silly. Look, let's stick to the protest."

"T-Diddy could have any girl at this party. Real talk."

"You can have every girl at this party, but you won't have this one. Real talk."

And then homegirl gets back in her car and speeds off.

"Like I said, she's out of your league."

"C'mon, son, it ain't over till it's over," I tell Willie Mack. "Don't underestimate T-Diddy's game."

"Yeah, how's that game working out for you?"

"T-DiddyGotSomeMagicUpHisSleeveRight?"

"You gonna hypnotize her?" Willie Mack says sarcastically.

"You got jokes. Step five of the ladykilla playa playbook is a guaranteed bong bong!"

"I thought it was only three steps," Belafonte muses.

"Y'all know he makes this ish up as he goes along. Ain't no steps, and definitely ain't no playbook," Willie Mack says.

"Hate all you want, homeboy, but wait till you see what I got in store for homegirl next. It's about to be KFC three-piece time."

"LegsThighsAndBreasts," Fast Freddie hollers, and we all laugh.

"Oh, snap! The DJ is going old school. 'Brooklyn rocks to the planet,'" I sing, trying to change the subject. As much as I want to believe that I still got this thing under control, Willie is right. Not only did I just piss her off, but this playa is out of moves.

"YoWeWasQuietForLikeTheWholeFirstBellOnFriday. That'sCrazy!"

"What's crazy is you did all this to dip in that honey," Willie Mack adds.

Yeah, that's how it started. I was trying to impress her, at first. But now I'm kind of into it. I mean, I'm not trying to change the world or nothing like that, but stuff does need to be different at our school.

Last week I was in the library for the first time all year. Half the shelves are empty. Claudia says we're supposed to have at least fourteen thousand books, but we only have three thousand. That's just wrong.

And now the administration is considering putting in metal detectors to curb the violence. So we're prisoners now. How do I say any of this on a Friday night to my boys while we're getting ready to get our party on? Buzzkill.

"I did it for a bunch of reasons, dawg. I'm a complex

individual. T-Diddy got many sides. I'm like an isosceles triangle."

Nobody says anything—they just stare at me. Finally we all bust out laughing.

"Well, I hope it works, 'cause West Charleston ain't the same without the marching band. Real talk."

The music stops for a second, and I hear my ears and my phone ring. I pull it out, thinking it's probably Uncle Al telling me to stop by the store and pick up something for him. But it's not. Six new text messages and two voice-mails. From Claudia Clarke.

"Fellas, I'll be back." I jump up to go.

"WhereYouGoingT? ThePartyJustStarting."

"Willie, give me your keys. I need to take care of something."

"It's on E, put some gas in that joint, T," he says, throwing me the keys.

Claudia

My sister is at work. I called Blu like seven times. No way was I calling my ex. He'd probably think it was an excuse to see him again. The only person left was Omar.

"Just admit it, you wanted to see me," he says, looking up at me.

Not. "That was just such an immature guy thing to do."

"I said I was sorry, dang."

"So I'm supposed to just up and accept your apology."

"Yep, if you want me to change this tire."

"Can you fix it?" I ask him, shivering. "It's getting colder out here."

"If you keep the flashlight steady, yeah. And I'm the one down here on the freezing ground," he answers. "You really should learn how to change a tire."

"That's why I have triple-A roadside assistance."

"A lot of good triple-A roadside assistance is doing you right now, homegirl."

I didn't intentionally let my membership expire. Senior year has been a challenge, with all the college applications, my projects, the newspaper, and now the protest. I really need to get my focus back.

"I wasn't going to pay them four hundred dollars to change a frickin' tire."

"So you called me."

"Yeah."

"You know, freedom ain't free, homegirl."

"Ha ha!"

Something about the way he smiles and the left side of his upper lip curls when he says "homegirl" always makes me almost smile. An hour ago, Omar Smalls was grabbing my ass, literally, with his muscular fingers. Now those same hands are changing my flat tire.

"Why is it taking you so long? It's just a tire? Jeez."

"Stop playing all hard and just admit that you like me."

"Random!"

"Claudia, you're cool. And I'm cool, so I don't understand why we can't just cool out together."

"Maybe because I'm chillin'," I respond, wishing I had worn a jacket to the party instead of trying to look so fly.

"Real funny. It's all good, though, I know you're kinda feeling me. I could tell by the way you put my arms around you on the dance floor tonight."

"I just did that to make Kym jealous."

"And that's why you put your tongue in my mouth the other night?" He looks up at me again, with the whole curly upper lip thing.

"I really don't want to talk about this. Are you almost finished, Omar?"

He goes back to twisting and unscrewing, and we are silent for way too long.

"So you'll be cool if I start dating Kym again?"

"It is what it is, Omar."

"So you're cool?"

"You can date anybody you want. Just remember it's a two-way street, homeboy." Why did I say that? Geeesh!

"Two-way street? Oh, so you *are* feeling me?"

"Never mind."

"Homegirl, I left the party to help your butt out. I was hanging with my boys, minding my own business. So it seems to me you owe T-Diddy."

"Owe you?"

"There's always consequences and repercussions."

"And what might they be?" I ask. Omar stands up, takes off his Panther jacket, puts it around me, then grabs my hand. "Oh, so now you want to be a gentleman. I could have frozen my butt off." Please don't try to kiss me again, please don't.

"Anyway, stop complaining. I've felt your butt, and it's pretty hot," he says, and we both can't help but laugh.

"First you snatch a kiss, then you grab my butt. Let me find out you're a criminal."

"A smooth criminal. Next, T-Diddy's gonna steal your heart," he says, not looking at me, which is good, because I don't want my swoon to encourage him. "And then I'm going to carry it right here." He looks at me, pounds his fist over his heart. "Homegirl, you okay?"

"Please, I'm fine."

"I know you're fine, but are you okay?" Do not smile, Claudia. Do not. "That was e.e. cummings, in case you didn't know."

"I know that. His words, your words don't faze me, homeboy," I lie, and try to pretend like e.e. cummings isn't one of my favorite poets and "i carry your heart with me" isn't my favorite frickin' poem. Ever.

"Then for the last time, please, hold the flashlight

straight? You're killing me, Claudia." He smiles and resumes changing my tire. "You owe me one night."

"What? Are you out of your mind? I already told you, I'm not going out with you."

"Hole up, homegirl, I wasn't talking about a date. Just a quick walk, tonight. That's all." I look down the street.

"What, like a walk around the block? Sure, no problem."

He stands up. "Hole up, hole up! You're getting a little too comfortable in my jacket, homegirl," he says. I look down at the jacket. When did all the buttons get snapped? "It looks good on you, though." I snatch his phone before he snaps a picture of me.

"You sure are dragging this out. Do you even know how to change a tire?"

"Are we going for a walk or not?"

"I said sure. Around the block."

"The block is cool, but I really need to clear my mind. Only one place can do that."

What, the mall? How romantic.

"Let's go down to Folly Beach."

"You're still talking about the beach. What, are you insane? It's the middle of the frickin' winter. Not in this lifetime." Omar slowly starts unbuttoning the jacket. His jacket. What are you doing? "Uh, what are you doing?"

"I'm leaving."

"But we're not finished. Hello!"

"T-Diddy is finished. Maybe you can get it finished next lifetime." No he didn't.

"Really, Omar? You're not going to fix my car unless I walk on the beach with you? That's so low." He's got a few more buttons to go.

"Everything is not about you, Claudia. I just have a lot on my mind with the protest and school and football. It's just one little walk."

"You can walk by yourself."

"I could, but I don't have a ride. I need to get Willie his car back like ASAP."

"Who goes walking on the beach in January? That's just crazy."

"Be in the now, Claudia," quoting something I heard Clyfe say once.

"I'll think about it," I tell him. Not.

I guess he doesn't want to really piss me off, because he leaves the jacket intact and gets back down on his knees. I'm not a shallow girl, but watching his arms jack up my car is, um, nice.

"Focus, please. Flashlight," he says. "I got a question. What happens if we get suspended?"

"They can't suspend the whole student body."

"True."

"Plus, we're not really causing trouble or breaking rules. This silent protest is really quite clever."

"Yeah, I thought the same thing when I came up with the idea," he says, and looks up at me, smiling again. I can't help but smile back.

"You didn't come up with the idea."

"Uh, yeah, I did."

"I take it you've never heard of Gene Sharp."

"Who?"

"We learned about him in government class. Civil disobedience, nonviolent stuff."

"You mean Dr. King," he says.

"Yeah, but Dr. King actually learned nonviolence from Gene Sharp."

"Well, I'd love to listen to your little lecture, professor, but I'm done. Spare tire is on."

"Great."

"Don't ride too far on this spare," he says, packing all of my tools and my busted tire in the trunk.

"I'm going out of town tomorrow."

"Where are you going?" he asks, sounding like my father.

"I'm going to mind my own business."

"My bad, I was just wondering because you should probably get the tire fixed and take this spare off if you're going too far. Take this joint to the shop first thing tomorrow, and see if they will patch it up for you."

"Okay, cool."

"For real, you gone all weekend?"

"If you must know, I'm visiting my aunt and uncle in Columbia."

"That's what's up. You want some company?"

"I'm good. Thanks a lot for coming out here to help me, Omar."

"Text me when you get in," he adds, then blows me a kiss and walks back to his car. A phone rings. I don't remember it's his until I've already answered.

"Hello," I say. Omar spins around, coming back toward me. A woman answers. Probably one of his chickens.

"Give me the phone, Claudia," he mouths.

"Omar's not here right now, may I take a message?" He tries to grab the phone from me, but I push him away. "Who's calling?" I run to the other side of the car. "Lucky what . . . huh? Oh, okay . . . not leaving tomorrow . . . yes, I will let him know. . . . Why you looking all worried, Omar?" I ask as I hang up.

"Huh? Who was it?"

"Don't worry, it wasn't one of your hootchy mamas."

"Stop playing, girl, and give me my phone." He throws his arms around me, almost lifting me off the ground, and snatches the phone. "Who was it?"

"I had no idea, Omar Smalls."

"What are you talking about?"

"Lucky Dog Animal Rescue."

"Oh, snap, that's tomorrow. Dang, I almost forgot."

"You volunteer with them. I'm shocked."

"Whatever."

"A lady named Ms. Williams—"

"Ms. Wilson," he corrects me.

"Yeah, well, she said the dogs aren't leaving tomorrow for Washington, D.C. It'll be in two days."

"That's what's up. Them dogs is my dawgs!" We both laugh. "I hope they all find homes up there in Chocolate City," he adds, looking as sincere as I've ever seen him.

"Why you didn't tell me you do volunteer work?"

"I didn't tell you I can recite the Declaration of Independence, either."

"You can?"

"No, silly. Be safe, I'm outta here."

"Yeah, you too, Omar Smalls."

Get in the car, Claudia. I'm standing in the middle of the street, still wearing his letterman's jacket. The easy thing to do is to get in the car, go home, work on my physics homework, and eat ice cream. Get in the car, Claudia. Omar Smalls is a player and a playa. A below average student, and as shallow as dirty pond.

And he rescues dogs.

Omar starts the car and flashes his lights at me. He pulls up beside me.

"You miss me already, don't you?"

"Whatever!" I roll my eyes. "Seriously, thanks for helping me."

"T-Diddy knows how to treat a special lady. Have a good night." He starts rolling up the window.

The easy thing to do is to let him drive off, go back with his boys, let some freaky freshman girl do the splits for him.

"Wait! Omar, wait!"

I'm afraid to really say what I am thinking. I don't want to become another box for him to check off. It's not like I like him. I don't, really. I'm sure it would feel great in his arms. To walk hand in hand under the moon, yadda yadda yadda. Yes, we might have a connection. A thing. But I really don't have time for any nonsense. Get in your car, Claudia.

"What is it, Claudia?" Nothing, never mind. "Well, it's getting cold, homegirl. So just keep the jacket. I'll pick it up when you get back to town." He does the whole curly upper lip thing. Very smooth, Omar. Very frickin' smooth.

"So now you're just going to leave me by myself," I say. "I thought we were going to the beach."

OMAR

"I hope you put some gas in Betty," Willie Mack yells.

"IThoughtWeWereGoingToTheMidnightMovieT," Fast Freddie screams. I rush out of the party, trying to get to homegirl before she changes her mind. And these jokers are following me.

"Pick me up for the gym tomorrow, Willie," I yell.

"I thought you were going to D.C."

"New plans. Same time. I'll holla," I say when I reach homegirl's ride.

"OhSnapThat'sClaudiaClarke.WillieThisWoadieIsDissingUsForClaudiaClarke!" Before I can shut the door, Willie and Fast Freddie are over at her window.

"What's new, Claudia?"

"Hey there, Willie. Hey, Fast Freddie!"

Fast Freddie starts cackling. He runs away from the car like he just won the lottery or something, screaming "BongBong!"

"What does that mean, Omar?" Claudia says, looking at me.

"Freddie can be so immature," I say. That joker is wildin' out. "Let's ride."

"Hole up, hole up, where y'all lovebirds going?"

"It's not like that, Willie. Omar and I are just friends."

As much as I want to tell him we're going to the beach, the last thing I need is for the whole football team to know my biz. I can just hear it now: "Awwwww, T-Diddy and Claudia took a late-night skinny dip on Folly."

"She's just giving me a ride home. I'll holla, Willie." I motion to Claudia to start the car.

"Willie, you should come over—T-Diddy's making omelets," homegirl says, giggling.

"That's what's up. Let me go and get the fellas, and we'll follow you," Willie Mack says, excitedly, then jets.

"Gas it, homegirl." I start the car for her in case she doesn't think T-Diddy is serious as a heart attack. "Let's do this."

* * *

"This is insane. I can't believe we're doing this."

"More insane than starting a schoolwide protest that has now spread across the city to other schools?"

"That's different."

"Whatever. I just want you to see something."

"See what?"

"The lighthouse."

"Uh, I can't see the lighthouse. It's pitch black," she says, pointing into the distance. "Now can we get back in the heated car?"

"We have to get up close to see it."

"WHAT? I'm not walking way down there. It's at the end of the frickin' island."

"I didn't know you were such a complainer. Can we just live in the moment?"

Jeez! "It's dark and scary, Omar. Crazy! This is so crazy!"

"C'mon now. T-Diddy will protect you from the, uh, crabs." I laugh just long enough for her to punch me in the arm.

Next to the ocean, it feels like forty degrees. Of all days not to wear socks. We're so close to the water, my feet are squishing. My toes are ice cubes, and homegirl is mighty cozy in her gloves and my jacket.

"Maybe we should go back," she says after we've been walking for a few minutes in silence. "You look a little cold."

"Naw, I'm good. But I'd be better if you were a little closer." I playfully pull her to me and stumble, almost falling into the water.

"You're not getting in my car all wet. Mess around and fall, you'll be walking back to Charleston."

"You know they say that two bodies can create instant heat."

In the distance, I see a figure approaching us. This apparently scares homegirl, because she inches closer to me. I put her arm inside mine, and she doesn't move it. The guy passes us by. "T-Diddy won't let anybody chop you up and throw you in the ocean."

"What are you doing, Omar?" She pulls her arm back and punches me again.

"What happened to nonviolent resistance? I'm not the enemy," I tell her, and take my shoes off. After I roll my jeans up to my knees, I slowly run ahead of her, splashing my feet in the water and hating every ice-cold minute of it.

"Omar, wait for me. Omar!" She runs and catches up to me. When she gets close, I turn around and pick her up. "Omar. OMAR, WHAT ARE YOU DOING?"

"Shhhhh! Before someone thinks you're in real trouble

or something." I hold her in my arms, far above the water, and walk till the ocean is right at my calves.

"Put me down, now!"

"Okay," I say, and start lowering her.

"NO, NOT HERE, OMAR!" she screams. "Take me back to the shore," she says in the sweetest voice.

"Kiss me first."

"Omar, stop playing. We could die right here. This water is frickin' below zero."

"Stop exaggerating, homegirl. A little piece of ocean won't hurt you," I say, and drop one arm long enough to splash her with a little water. She doesn't open her mouth when she screams, but the sound is loud as thunder. Believe that! "I bench press more than you fifty times a day. I got you, homegirl."

"But you can't stop the waves. If a big enough one comes, we could both fall in."

Love. The moon shows me her eyes, and they are magnets pulling me closer to her. Kiss her, Omar. Do it.

"Omar, I got to pee."

"Good thing we're in the ocean, huh, homegirl?"

Uncle Al and I come to Folly to fish a lot, sometimes at night. Spooky and Clyfe join us sometimes. We sit on the pier at nine, ten o'clock at night. They drink beer, and I listen to them jokers try to one-up each other with stories about women they've dated and cars they've owned. Hardly any fishing takes place, but every time they start arguing about random ish like whether South Carolina ought to have an NFL team, or who's better looking, Michelle Obama or Oprah Winfrey, it's worth the trip. Good times.

Later on, I started coming at night, alone, during the off-season to train. I'd start at one end of the beach and run all the way to the lighthouse. It was pitch black, and since the lighthouse wasn't lit, I relied on the moon.

But my favorite time is when the whole Lucky Dog crew brings the dogs to run around, play in the water. Love to see them having fun and being free.

Nothing distracts me—not girls, not Facebook, not homework. I'm focused, at peace, and in tune with the rhythm of the ocean.

Claudia isn't the first girl I've brought here at night. Believe that, for sure. This is where T-Diddy closes the deals.

I walk us back to the shore, the waves still crashing into my legs. I place her down in the sand.

"Who does that?" She's obviously a little perturbed. "These gloves are useless. I can't even feel my hands."

"Look." I point at the moon. "We'll use it as our guide."

"Oh, so now you're Harriet Tubman," she says, taking off her gloves and putting them in her pocket.

"We're almost there. Come on, Claudia, let's walk." We got out of the ocean just in time. Several large waves smash into the shore. The sound is beautiful and haunting.

"It's hard to even know where it all begins and ends. It's just so dark. And big."

"That's what she said." And she punches me again. "Seriously, for me, it begins with Claudia Clarke," I add, stopping and turning to face her. "For me, a dark place is a bad place without you. Yes, I want to kiss you." And *smash*. "But right now what I really want to do is hold your hand. Is keep you warm." Is surrender to the wave that is crashing into my heart. "Is that possible, homegirl?"

Look out, the ladykiller strikes again.

Claudia

"For me, it begins with Claudia Clarke," he says. My eyes are finally used to the darkness. The stars are ablaze and his face is in the center of the light. "For me, a dark place is a bad place without you. Yes, I want to kiss you. But right now what I really want to do is hold your hand. Is that possible, homegirl?" I can't tell if he's for real or not.

I don't drink, but I'm a little intoxicated at the moment. The moon, the water, the sound of the ocean, everything has got me. Even the way he says "homegirl" all sexy and confident is starting to grow on me. Jeez. I didn't think I liked him. I mean, he's cute and we have a good time together, and the silent protest and yadda yadda yadda. Still, he's a playa.

C'mon, Claudia. Did he really go through all this to get with you?

This jock who loves carrying a ball more than anything has somehow become a leader. Together, we've changed the way kids in our school think. The closest these kids would ever come to culture is bacteria. But he and I are changing that. We're a team. Really, Claudia. Don't be stupid.

Mr. Football has somehow become my tire-changing savior. My late-night-on-the-beach, dog-rescuing leader. And I kinda like it.

I like the way he smells. I like the way he walks, all confidently, head reaching for the moon. I like the way the diamond in his ear shines. I even like the way he carried me into the frickin' ocean. And I really like that he just asked me could he hold my hand. But there's no way that I like this guy. There's just no way. I think. I need rehab.

He takes my silence for a yes and pulls my freezing-cold hand out of my pocket and places his fingers between mine. How is it that his fingers are so warm?

"Wow, you are cold-blooded," he says, doing the curly lip thing again.

"I can't believe we're doing this."

"You want to hear a story?" he asks as we continue

walking toward the lighthouse. My hand gets lost in his. I'm a little worried that this is feeling so comfortable. Too good.

"As long as it isn't scary, sure."

"It might be a little scary, so hold on tight," he says. Any tighter and he might get the wrong idea. I'm staying right where I am, Omar.

"Once upon a time, there was a farmer and his wife, who lived in a mansion. He had two assistants to look after his livestock and vegetable and flower gardens. The assistants also lived on the farm with their families. Aside from the farm, the farmer's main responsibility was watching over a tower that was adjacent to his farm.

"The story goes that the tower was once a lighthouse built in the 1700s by King George the Third."

"I didn't know you were a history buff, Omar."

"Just listen to the story, homegirl."

I like the way you call me that.

"Anyway, like I was saying before I was rudely interrupted. It was replaced by a bigger and better one that was built in the 1800s. The lighthouse was used by the Confederate soldiers during the Civil War to alert them to approaching Union soldiers."

It's starting to get warmer.

"The lighthouse was also used by a slave during the Civil War. This dude was working on a military ship called the *Planter*. The ship had all kinds of military cargo—guns, ammunition, and whatnot. Anyway, the *Planter*'s three white officers decided to spend the night ashore, drinking and chasing women in Chucktown. So when they left, the slave got this grand idea. He was gonna escape, get as far away from his Confederate masters as possible. So he and about eight other enslaved crewmen decided to make a run for it. This dude was no joke. He put on a captain's uniform and had a straw hat similar to that of the white captain, and he piloted the ship."

How are both of our hands clasped, and why does it feel like someone turned up the heat on the inside?

"First they picked up their families, then this joker piloted the *Planter* past the five Confederate forts that guarded Charleston Harbor. He used the lighthouse as a beacon, the silver moon as his GPS, and made it to the Union ships, where he turned over everything to the soldiers, including a Confederate codebook that helped the North win the war."

"Wait a minute, Omar. This story sounds familiar, like something I'd read about in AP History class. You stealing again?"

"The lighthouse ended up being destroyed in the war, but it got rebuilt for a third time. And this time, a farmer was put in charge of making sure that nothing happened to it."

I squeeze his hand tighter; playfully bend myself a little into him. And stay there. I do this without thought. It feels so natural.

"Well, one day, the farmer's wife, who he loved very much—I think her name was Claudia."

"No, it wasn't," I say, and punch him in the stomach. "Seriously, is this story for real?"

"As real as it gets, homegirl," he says, and grabs me even tighter and closer than we were before. It may as well be eighty degrees out here. "Not so cold anymore, huh?" he says, wiping my forehead with his palm. How am I sweating?

"Anyway, like I was saying, the farmer comes home and sees his wife in the lighthouse staring off into the distance. He immediately goes up to the top of the lighthouse to see what she's looking at." Omar pauses, and for a moment I feel a soft wind blow in my ear. It's either him or the ocean, both of which are close to owning me right now.

"They see a storm coming. Only it's not just any old storm. It's a typhoon."

"Really, Omar. A frickin' typhoon in Charleston."

"Or a hurricane. The point is, it's huge. And it destroys the mansion, the homes of the farmer's assistants, the livestock, everything. It's complete devastation. Over time, the land around the tower disappears. So now it sits in the middle of the ocean, surrounded by water on all sides."

I'm standing on the beach, in his arms, and it just feels right. We're so close to the water, I can taste the salt in the air. Every now and then a large wave brings a splash of cold near enough that my ankles and legs should flinch. But they don't. I am on fire, somewhere inside. And the only thing I feel right now is too good.

"What happened to the farmer and his wife?" I ask.

"Rumor has it that they are still up there," he says in a macabre voice, trying to scare me.

"Stop, Omar. That's not funny."

"Seriously, the lighthouse hasn't been lit in over a hundred and fifty years, but if you come out here at night, sometimes you can see a glow coming from it. Look," he says, and points just over the dunes. "We're here. There it is."

"Wow, I've never seen it at night."

"Best time to see it is now. This is exactly how the slaves saw it when they were escaping. What do you think?"

"I think it's a beautiful story. And I also think you made a lot of it up."

"Actually, it's mostly true. Uncle Al told me the story." He lets me go from his embrace and sits down on the sand. I'm still staring at the lighthouse, feeling surreal. "Aren't you going to sit down?"

"Omar, what are you doing?" I ask, turning around to look down at him. I don't want to be hurt. "Please tell me you didn't bring me out here, tell me all this stuff, just so you can sleep with me."

"Look, you know I'm feeling you, and I can tell that even though you may not want to, you kinda feeling me."

"Don't play games with me, Omar." He pulls my arm, and my butt lands next to him in the sand.

"About fifteen years ago," he continues, "an organization called Save the Light bought the lighthouse from the state of South Carolina. They're doing a lot to protect it, but it's our responsibility as well, just like it was the farmer's and his wife's."

"Protect it from what?"

"From beach erosion. It leans more and more each year. Before you know it, it'll be underwater, and a part of our history will be lost," he says passionately. "Claudia, this lighthouse is powerful, it's really amazing. It has survived wars, hurricanes, even earthquakes. And it's still standing. Save the Light has raised millions of dollars to restore it. To preserve it from being lost to the sea."

"Hmmm, sounds a little suspect to me. With all the money they raised, how many homeless people could they have fed? It's a little elitist, don't you think?"

"What I think is everybody has their purpose, their mission. One person helps feed the homeless, and another protects a historic landmark from erosion. Somebody raises money to save chimpanzees, while another group of people rescues dogs. Whether you're occupying Wall Street or starting a schoolwide protest at your high school, there are different ways to change the world, homegirl. We all walk our own path, right?" Yes, Omar, YES! Before I can agree, he turns me around. I open my mouth to protest.

"Shhhhhhhhh!" He puts his finger to my lips.

"The dude that stole the ship during the Civil War and freed like thirty slaves, that woadie was no joke. I might be the best football player in the country, but I ain't got nothing on that joker. The Army made him a major general and even named a ship after him. The U.S.S. *Robert Smalls*." I knew it sounded familiar. We'd read about Robert Smalls in history classes for the past four years. Pilot, captain, and politician, he was best known for . . . wait a minute. Wait one minute. Robert SMALLS!

"Omar, are you saying—"

"Yep, my great-great-great-grandfather was Robert Smalls."

I don't know how or when it happens, but both of my sweaty hands are clinched in his. He pulls me closer, so now my butt rests on his loglike thighs. My eyes are transfixed on his eyes. He is a few words away from owning me. Funny how what someone says and what you want them to say can sometimes get all crossed up.

What he actually says next is: "I ain't perfect like this beach, and yeah, I might be a star football player, and the ladies love T-Diddy, but I ain't dumb and I know a thing or two about changing the world too, homegirl. So why don't you give me a chance, Claudia Clarke?"

What I hear, though, is: "This beach and me. We're one, Claudia. I've been coming here for almost two years. *Two years*. But it never dawned on me that it was meaningful. That the lighthouse was significant. That it has a story, an important one. Until now. Until this very moment. Until you helped me understand that it does matter. That everything matters. Without the lighthouse, I wouldn't be here. Literally. It gave my grandfather, and his father and his father, and his father, and me life. And you've given me a new one. Homegirl, you have been my lighthouse. I've followed you these past few weeks and found a power I didn't know I possessed. What good is a voice if you don't use it to speak up?"

In this moment, there is no more silent protest. There is no band or dance or newspaper. These things are on hold. There is no more "I only date college guys," and certainly no more "I'm not interested in Omar Smalls." Each of these things belongs to a different girl in a different time, before this moment.

In this moment, I am a new girl, unafraid, drowning in desire, and dashing to dive in.

"Slow down, homegirl," he whispers.

But I can't. This is where I want to be. Inside his arms. Beneath the silver moon.

I toss my jacket, which is his, behind us. He gently unbuttons my shirt, while I lift his above the concrete shoulders that have won championships. And the whole time, we don't say a single word. Still, his unbroken gaze speaks volumes of unspoken words:

Give me a chance, Claudia.

Let me show you who I really am, Claudia.

I promise I won't hurt you, Claudia.

174

For him, kissing seems as easy as throwing a pass. Or swimming. He takes his time, navigating the curve of my lips with his. Lips. Tongue. Oh my!

I am not so gentle. Like a frenzied shark, I quickly take the whole of him. Biting, bending, craving each and every kiss.

"Girl, just relax. I got you. Ain't no army coming after you," he says, and laughs.

I surrender. He runs his scorching fingers through my hair. I hold his breath in mine. His eyes take me in. And I no longer fear the wave coming.

It is here.

OMAR

Tdiddy Smalls C'mon son, why is Willie Mack in here blasting Pink? Put that Meek Mill on. #PumpingIron
Like · Comment · Share · @DaRealTdiddy · Saturday at 7:30 am ·

Usually Fast Freddie works out with us, but this joker calls me coughing at five thirty this morning.

"IGotTheFluOrSomethingT."

"You're suspect, dawg." He coughs in the phone, like I don't know he and Belafonte just got in a few hours ago. Jokers always hiding and trying to be all secretive about their ish, and then they put it on Facebook. C'mon, son. "Same ol' party and bullshit. Y'all need to get your priorities straight," I tell him.

"TrueTrue. TDidYouSmash?"

Click.

Willie Mack and I are the only ones in the gym. We've been in here for about an hour.

"How come they never turn the heat on in this joint on weekends?" he asks, his sweat dripping on me while he spots my bench press. "Hurry up, dawg, I'm hungry."

It's hard to think about food or heat or anything else up in here. My mind is on one thing.

Last night, Claudia and I were sitting on Folly Beach at midnight. We walked. We kissed. It wasn't anybody else on the beach but the two of us. She grabbed my hand and slid her fingers in between mine. The rest of the night was like a dream.

"What number is that?" I ask, grunting while struggling to lift the three-hundred-pound weights off my chest for the tenth time.

"Focus, T. Stop thinking about ol' girl and focus."

"Ain't nobody thinking about her," I grunt.

"Then why you didn't hang out with us last night? Why you don't eat lunch with us no more?"

WTF!

"You ain't even watch the game with us on Sunday? You always on her FB?" he says, pressing the bar down.

"C'mon, Willie, stop pressing so hard." He lets up a little.

"You sound like a little bish. Stop tripping." Truth was, he wasn't really tripping. I hadn't really thought about how much time I was spending with homegirl.

"I got your bish," he says, gritting on me, pressing the bar down with all his might. It takes every ounce of strength I have to keep it off my neck. "It's the last one. C'mon now, push."

"Then let up, dayum!" When I finally get the barbell up, he takes it and places it on the stand.

"Willie Mack, I'm just having fun with ol' girl. You know how T-Diddy does."

"I hear ya talking, woadie," he says sarcastically.

"C'mon son. T-Diddy is all about dropping the panties. Don't get it twisted," I say, not even believing myself.

"A'ight, dawg. I'm all about Panera. Let's hit it."

"I'm taking a shower first, and you should too."

"I'm good. I'll be out here, but I ain't waiting forever. Hurry up, before they run out of soufflé. That spinach artichoke joint is the truth."

I'm in the shower for almost fifteen minutes, just letting the water hit me before I even begin to clean off the funk. I can't stop thinking about homegirl.

What I really want to do is see Claudia, tell her I think I love her. It sucks that she's in Columbia. I'm not even in the mood for Panera. I just want to go home, make me an omelet, some turkey bacon, and watch college football. By myself. Maybe she'll call.

I get out the shower and hear Rick Ross coming from the speakers.

"It's about time you put on some real playa music, homeboy," I scream out to Willie Mack as I check myself out in the mirror. Look at those muscles. T-Diddy's arms are ripped. I wrap myself in the orange-and-green beach towel I got on my first recruiting trip to the U.

After drying myself off, I drape the towel over my locker and stare at the big UM logo. A few more months and I'm gonna be a Hurricane. I can't wait for that ish. Can't nobody stop T-Diddy. I hope there aren't any hidden cameras in here, 'cause Nicki Minaj is blasting now and I'm dancing naked on the floor. At least until Willie Mack cuts it off.

"Mack, why you cut that jam off? C'mon son," I shout at him from the locker room.

I'm feeling so good, I decide that I'm gonna text homegirl, maybe ask her something about the protest. Make it official, so she doesn't think I'm pushing up on her too hard. I hear Willie Mack walking in from the weight room.

"Willie Mack, look at this." I flex my arms. "I think I'm

bigger than yesterday."

"Yeah, definitely bigger," a female voice says. I turn around, and standing a few lockers away, staring at me standing naked, is none other than Kym King. "Hey, T-Diddy, what you doing?"

"WHOA! I'm working out. Where's Willie Mack?"

"Yeah, I can see you hard at work," she says, smiling and walking toward me till I can smell her watermelon bubble gum. "He left, said something about Waffle House."

"Panera."

"Yeah, that too. I see you're happy to see me," she says, and slaps my ass. I pull her into me without even thinking. C'mon son, watchu doing?

"Me wanna ride."

"Girl, somebody could come in." Get it together, T-Diddy. I back away. An inch or so. "Kym, I'll holla at you later."

"Let me ride T-Diddy's whip."

"This ain't cool." Even though it does feel hella good. "How you even know I was here?"

"Uh, you're here every Saturday, silly." She was right about that. "Plus you put it on Facebook."

"Look, Kym, I don't—" and then she kisses me and reminds me why I started dating her in the first place. She got a supersize tongue, and she knows how to work that joint.

Before I know it, my hands are around her waist again, this time, grinding. She's moaning, I'm groaning, and it's about to go down. Game on!

T-Diddy drops back to his locker. Checks out the field. Kym rushes him. Drops down to her knees. He's got the ball. Fumble. Now she's got it. What will she do with it. OH MY!

"Ohhh, yes, uh, oh, bong bong, no, uh, protect—, oh, Claudia," I say, my hand cradling her weave.

"What the hell?" Kym pushes away from me.

"Why you stopping, Kym?"

"What did you just say?"

"I said I didn't have any protection, but it's no big deal, I can run out to the 7-Eleven and grab some plastic."

"No, what name did you call me, T-Diddy?"

What name did I call her? I didn't know what she was talking about, but it was just like Kym to trip out on some inconsequential ish. I was kinda in the moment. Maybe I called her a B.

"You got me all vertical. Why you wildin' out?"

"'Cause you called me that trick. Claudia."

Claudia. I did not call her . . . oh, snap, I did. I called her Claudia.

"It was just jokes, Kym," I say, trying to calm her down

so we can get back to business.

"You dating her?"

"Uh, naw, not really, we're just friends." Which was the truth, we were still friends, according to Claudia. Maybe close friends.

"Not really is the best you can do?"

"We're working on the silent protest together. It's complicated," I say, pulling the towel down and wrapping it around myself.

"I don't even know why you're wasting your time on her and that stupid protest. It ain't gonna change ish."

"It's already changed something. Have you seen the way it's been less fights in school, and everybody's acting like we a community of students?"

"A community? Omar, what the hell are you talking about? Don't nobody care about changing our school. Claudia got your head all blowed up thinking you Malcolm X or something."

"Ain't nobody got T-Diddy's head blown up. I believe in what we're doing. It may not change the world, but it's gonna change the world right here at West Charleston. Believe that!"

"That's funny," she says, laughing. "T-Diddy Smalls trying to change the world, and I thought you was just trying to get in Claudia's pants."

"Whatever, Kym."

"Yeah, everybody knows about your bet with Willie Mack and 'em. He told my girl Tisha, who told her sister Renee, who's dating my brother, who told me. Why you even want that stuck-up B when you can have all this?" she says, inching closer to me. "Just don't call me by her name again. That ish is foul," she adds, kissing on my chest. "So is it gonna be me or her, Omar?"

You know how people say they know exactly where they were at the exact moment their life changed forever? My uncle Al says he was at the corner store buying pork rinds and sweet potatoes when Dr. Martin Luther King, Jr., was shot. Our government teacher says he was at the Charleston Grill listening to jazz when President Obama got elected. Fast Freddie said he was watching *Sesame Street* when his momma came screaming in the house that Tupac was dead. Until last night and today, I never had one of those moments.

I'm standing here naked, staring at this dope-looking chick who is ready to give me what I want, and all I have to do is tell her what she wants to hear. To tell her what I've told every other girl who I wanted to get with: "You are the center of my galaxy." But I can't. Because there is another

Venus in my orbit. And even though it feels like she is a universe away, I miss her. I can't think of anything but her. Her smile. Her words. Her skin. Her kiss. Everything else is alien. What the fug am I talking about? Get it together, T-Diddy. Smash Kym.

"Her," I answer, and back away. "We're done here, Kym. Deuces."

"I hope those Bayside boys beat your punk ass down," she says, and storms away. All I can do is laugh at how random that is. "I got your laughter, T-Diddy. Believe that."

I pull out my phone to see if I have any missed calls. Fast Freddie texts me twice to see if he can come over for omelets. Willie Mack texts to ask me where we're watching the Miami game and to bring his iPod. Uncle Al wants me to drive all the way downtown to get him some potato soup from Five Loaves. Texts from them and everybody else. Everybody except Claudia.

Omar Smalls: Homegirl, thinking of you. Hope you're safe. I miss you

A few minutes later, I'm putting on my sneaks when I hear the most beautiful sound in the world. The ringtone that lets me know I have a new text. I've never been so happy to hear a *boing* in my life, except when Coach texted me about Miami's full athletic scholarship.

I don't know what I am expecting her to say: "Meet me in Columbia tonight; I need to see you ASAP. Last night was the best night of my life. I love you, T-Diddy." But what she texts back makes me smile and almost blows my mind.

Claudia Clarke: Moi aussi, mon ami

After Google translates the first two words, my heart leaps out of my chest. When I read the last two, it hits the floor. *Hard.*

Friends?

Claudia

The protest isn't working.

The bell rang ten minutes ago, and there was no silent protest. Everybody's in here talking, like normal. We're losing momentum. Maybe Omar's mad at me because I didn't call him when I got back last night. Maybe he's pissed off because we haven't talked since Folly Beach. Whatever.

We're on day eleven, and the situation is no better than when we started. The spring play auditions usually happen this week, but since there's no drama club, that's been canceled too. Cruella probably thinks she can wait us out; that we'll get complacent, give up on it. Not me. I'll ride this fight until the wheels fall off. As long as she doesn't follow up on that whole Harvard threat thing.

"Oh, snap, look at this," Belafonte screams from his seat near the window. Everyone, including Mr. Washington, looks out to see what he's gawking at.

There is a sea of white vans lined up in front of our school. Every TV station is represented. And not just the local ones. There's a CNN and a Fox truck. I chuckle to myself when I see the BET van.

"Mr. Washington, we're famous," says Tami, who had to take out her tongue ring because of an infection. Now I can understand what the heck she's saying, but I can't look at her.

"BET is in the house. We're gonna be on *106 & Park*, y'all," yells another student.

"What's this?" asks Mr. Washington.

"They're probably here for the protest," Belafonte says.

"I just hope the principal and the school board are listening," I say.

"Well, they'll certainly hear us now," Mr. Washington adds. I love the fact that he says "us."

"Hey, Claudia, why didn't we do the silent protest today?" says Tami.

Omar didn't post it on his Facebook, and it was too late to call when I got in at two in the frickin' morning.

Actually, it wasn't too late, but I really needed a break

from him, from whatever I was feeling. The weekend gave it to me. Maybe he's done with the silent treatment. Maybe Miami threatened to take his scholarship away if he continued. Maybe he just punked out. Maybe he's pissed. Maybe I'm trippin'.

"Claudia, what's the deal with the silent treatment?" Belafonte asks.

Now everybody's looking at me, even Mr. Washington. They want an answer. I'm sure the whole school does. Just as surely as Omar and I got the school amped up, we can lose 'em.

Omar's the popular guy, the friend to everybody, the face of our movement. This is what I've always known. Now it's really slapping me upside my head: Omar "T-Diddy" Smalls is our leader. And right now, I know as much about his plan as the rest of the school. Not good, Claudia.

"Claudia, what's up? Did you talk to Omar?" Belafonte asks.

"Well, what we are doing is very important, and I, uh, like all of you, I'm still fired up, and I can't take no more."

But, before I can finish, an announcement begins.

"What's up, Panthers?" says the voice over the loudspeaker. Is that . . . "It's your boy, T-Diddy."

In the background, we hear banging on a door and a

voice that sounds like Cruella herself. "Open this door now!"

"I gotta make this quick people, 'cause the Man is out to get me. First off, sorry I left y'all hanging on the silent treatment today, but T-Diddy was a little lovesick last night, and I didn't got a chance to tweet or post. Thas right, T-Diddy's in love."

My heart sinks right below my stomach and down near my toes. I hope he's not about to do what I think he's going to do. He's in love? Again, everybody's looking at me. Or at least it feels like it.

"Open your windows, Panthers. Let the newspeople hear our cries." Everyone looks at Mr. Washington, who nods, giving permission to open them. Belafonte and a few other boys do just that. Omar continues. "T-Diddy's in love with righteousness. T-Diddy's in love with freedom."

Whew! That was close. For a second I thought he was going to . . . uh, never mind. Reporters and guys with news cameras hoisted on their shoulders are now out of their vans, inching closer to the school.

"Second, we made our demands clear, but they still don't hear us. What do we want? We want band back. We want the choir back. We want dance, we want the drama club. We want all of the part-time teachers restored to full-time. That's what we want."

The cheers are raucous. Not just in our class, but all through the school. The sound of everyone clapping at the same time is thunderous. Boom mics from the TV people are pointed at the school.

"Mr. Smalls, open the door this minute or don't come in to school tomorrow," we hear Cruella scream, like the madwoman she is.

As much as I want him to keep on leading us, I really don't want him to get suspended.

"We gotta step up our game, people. Feel me. They thought five minutes a day was something, wait till they see how Panthers ride from now on. Starting tomorrow, we're gonna double it." The cheers are even louder this time. I'm getting that warm feeling again.

"That's two days' suspension, Mr. Smalls. Somebody break this lock, please," Dr. Jackson yells. Mr. Jensen is our school custodian. He's a real good man, but he's also got a very sick wife, and as much as I don't want him to break the lock on the door, I also know he needs to keep his job to take care of her.

"Just for that, let's put in some work now. When the bell rings, let 'em hear us. Feel me?" Yes, Omar, we feel you! "They can suspend me for a week or a year, it doesn't matter. These jokers can't suspend justice. T-Diddy's riding with y'all for life. Don't stop now, Panthers, we catchin' our stride," he finishes. This is the frickin' beach all over again. Jeez!

And then Omar plays a song over the loudspeaker, a reggae song that nobody but a few diehard ol' school music heads recognize. It doesn't matter, though, because the beat is fierce, and the words speak volumes:

> *Ain't nothin' gonna break my stride*
> *Nobody's gonna slow me down, oh no*

The next voice we hear is none other than Cruella's, and she's angrier than a Democrat in Texas.

"Teachers, this silent treatment nonsense is over. If any of your students participate, please let the front office know, and they will be suspended immediately. That is all. Good day." And then the bell sounds.

Everyone in class looks at each other. No one knows exactly what to do. Sure, we've been given our mission by our fearless leader, but nobody really wants to be suspended from school. Mr. Washington would never turn us in. Would he? I can't even imagine how that's going to go over with Harvard. Two things happen next that tell me what I should do.

First, Belafonte points at something outside. We get up to look and see Omar being escorted out of the school by the assistant principal. Cruella obviously was serious about suspending him. He gets to the sidewalk, where all the TV reporters are, and turns around to look back at the school. The way he scans the building lets me know that students in other classes are looking at him. He raises his hand in a balled fist, then slowly brings down his hand to his mouth and places his index finger to his mouth.

Second, when we go back to our seats, Mr. Washington removes his sweater to reveal a black T-shirt printed in white with six letters and an exclamation point:

SHHHHH!

I don't know if I love Omar Smalls, but today I've decided I really really really like him. Really.

OMAR

"These are for you," I say, and hand her a dozen multi-colored tulips.

"How sweet," she says, half sarcastically. I know you're feeling me, Claudia. She hugs me way past the normal three-second friendship hug. T-Diddy's about to score. Ten seconds later, she grabs my hand and pulls me into the house.

"Nice place. T-Diddy likes."

"Rule number one: if I'm going to help you with your paper, you must abandon the third person ish."

"No problem, T-Did— I mean, I understand," I say, still reeling from the potent hug. This girl has got my heart.

Her place is roomy and filled with religious paintings,

African masks, and books. It's like church in here.

"You sure have a lot of pictures of Jesus on the wall, Claudia."

"My parents are missionaries in Ghana."

"So, they're in Africa like, now?"

"Yeah, but don't get any ideas. My sister will be home soon, and plus we're just friends," she says, and grabs my hand for the first time since we were on the beach.

"I hear ya talking, Claudia."

"What's that supposed to mean?"

"Nothing." Our eyes have not left each other since I arrived, and I think we both know that tonight will be another special night. "It's just that you're still holding my hand." She tries to snatch it away, but I hold on tight. I don't want to rush things, so I let go. You got all night, Omar.

"Sorry you got suspended, Omar," she says, and walks into the kitchen. I follow her.

"No biggie. It is what it is," I say, borrowing her favorite line. Her smile makes me smile, and for a second we both stand in front of the fridge grinning like little kids about to get a Popsicle.

"The good thing is, with all the TV and newspaper coverage, they have to listen to us now."

"For sure, it's about to be on at West Charleston."

"And it's all because of you, Omar Smalls." What I hear next is "You want to get naked?" which sends my heartbeat racing. That was quick. But when she hands me the bottle of juice, I realize what she actually said was "You want a Naked?" as in organic juice. "Let's go into the living room and sit down."

"I heard the protest was banizzles today."

"If by banizzles, you mean frickin' awesome, then yeah, it was. Cru tried to get the teachers to report students who participated, but nobody did. It was crazy cool!"

"Willie Mack brought me a T-shirt after school. Those joints are fire. Who made them?"

"I don't even know, but Luther was selling them for ten dollars at lunch."

"The smoker kid."

"Yep."

"That's what's up," I say, and then she kisses me. Just like that, she kisses me. And I'm not talking about a sweet I'm-your-friend kind of peck either. One minute, she's on one end of the couch, I'm on the other, and we're talking about the protest. The next minute, her tongue is dancing down my throat. It happens that fast, like in the movies when the girl decides that she's going to go for it, let her guard down, and just kiss the guy. That's what Claudia does. She goes *Sideways*.

And then she stops. The only thing I can think to say is "That was random."

"Did you like it?"

"Uh, yeah, I, uh—"

"Wow, this is the first time I've heard T-Diddy speech-less. My kiss must be lethal."

Hole up—T-Diddy's confused. Homegirl is in control, and, uh, c'mon, son, get it together.

Claudia keeps on talking. "Look, Omar, I've been think-ing about you, me, and us."

"There's an us now?" I say, trying to grab my bearings back.

"The truth is, I do like you, Omar. I like the way you walk, the way you talk, the way you call me homegirl. I love the way you've turned our entire school around. Whenever I'm with you like this, I feel like a thief, like I just want to steal your lips. Hijack your heart and place it in a safe place. Right here." She grabs my hand, which is wiping the sweat from my forehead, and puts it on her breast.

There are things you want and you never get. And there are things you want and you get. But then there are things that you didn't know you wanted, and when you get them, you are so not prepared.

T-Diddy is not prepared for this. Three weeks ago, I just wanted to smash. Hell, three days ago, I thought all I wanted to do was smash. It's been so long since I really liked a girl, I don't even know how to do this. Don't have any rules or playbook or steps to follow. It's not nervousness I feel, more like anticipation. Like, I've been slowly moving up the steep hill, and now the roller coaster is about to go down. Real fast. And I'm in the front row. I'm just unprepared. Fortunately, I am saved by a knock on her front door.

"Aren't you going to get that?" I mumble, in between visits from her lips.

"It's probably my sister. She always knocks while she's looking for her keys in her bag. By the time I get there, she's coming in the door." She's still holding my hand over her heart. "You want your hand back, Omar?" Time to bong bong! This is what you wanted, homeboy. Let's do this.

There's the knock on the door again.

"Jeez, why is she so lazy?" Claudia gives me my hand back, and I don't know what to do with it. Now it feels foreign without a place to rest it. Without her. Stop acting like a little punk. You're a football star. "Hold that thought, Omar. I'll be right back."

I'm still roller-coaster excited, and it's not just because

I'm going get some tonight.

I wipe my forehead some more and take off my Miami sweatshirt. It's nearly drenched. I pull out my wallet. Please, have a condom. I do. Oh, snap, I just dropped it. I pick it up, inspect the package. Please don't be open. Then I drop it again. My phone vibrates. Who's texting me?

Uncle Albert: Bring some toilet paper home, Smalls.

I bend down to pick up the condom, and when I look up, she's back. And she's not alone.

"This is why you didn't want me to come in, Claudia?" some dude in a pink sweater says, looking like a fake Common in geek eyeglasses. He's taller than me, but only because he has dreadlocks.

"You can't be busting all up in my house. I'm busy," she shouts.

"Well, I can see that you're about to get busy," he says, smiling at me holding my condom. "You look familiar, dude." He moves his hair out of his face like he's been doing it all his life and just stares at me. "Wait a minute, you're that football player I saw on the news."

"T-Diddy Smalls, pardner," I say, in my best Brooklyn swagger.

"Y'all causing all that trouble at the school. We shall overcome and all that ish." He laughs. "Yeah, you s'posed to be a'ight with a ball."

"That's what they say, homeboy." Now I'm standing up.

"Going to Miami. So you think you can handle my girl Claudia, huh?"

"Leo, I'm not your girl anymore. Why are you tripping? Just leave, please," she says to him.

"I'ma go, I'm just messing with homeboy," he says, making quotes with his fingers when he says "homeboy." He turns around to leave, but I guess changes his mind because he looks back at me. "Look, pod-nuh," he adds, with the fingers again, "you might play football but Claudia's high class, Harvard bound, way too good for your slick city-boy routine. Why do you think you'd have a chance with her when she's already had someone like moi? Stick to throwing touchdowns."

"Nucka, you don't know me. You better check yourself before you wreck yourself," I say, walking to him. Claudia stands in between us, and for no reason, this clown starts laughing.

"Seriously, Claudia, *tu aimes ce type—vraiment*?" Here I was thinking this was going to blows, and he starts speaking French. College boy is a little lame. No wonder she dumped him.

"*Mais va t'en,*" she says to him. No she didn't just answer him in French. Now I feel really stupid, but T-Diddy ain't going out like that.

"I think Claudia wants you to leave, man. Real talk," I say, projecting the bass in my voice.

"*Non, ce n'est pas ton affaire!*" he says, and I know it's something foul 'cause he's gritting on me and pointing his finger at me. This would be the time for homegirl to make this joker leave, 'cause the next thing I say will be with my knuckles. She says something else to him in French. It's not good if I don't understand what you're saying, Claudia.

"Like I said, playa, stick to football," he says, and pokes me in the chest. Then, just as my dukes go up, Claudia spins around.

"Omar, I need to get some stuff that belongs to Leo. Just give us a few minutes."

What. The. Hell. Give you a few minutes? I shoulda smashed Kym when I had the chance.

"T-Diddy can do better than that. Take as many minutes as you want. *Au revoir!*" I grab my bag and walk toward the door.

"Omar, please don't go. I'm sorry." I pass the tulips on the way out, and wish I hadn't wasted that fifty dollars.

Should have treated her like all the rest of them tricks.

I get in Uncle Al's van and pray that this isn't one of the times it needs a jump.

"Boy, I kept switching the channel, trying to escape the ugly, but you was all up on my screen," Spooky says to me. He and Uncle Al and Clyfe are on the stoop again.

"Smalls is a big TV star now. Proud of my nephew."

"Thanks, Unc. We're gonna fight the power until they give us what we want."

"'Genius is the ability to act rightly without precedent—the power to do the right thing the first time,'" Clyfe quotes.

"Smalls, I think Clyfe just called you a genius."

"Well, you know how I do."

"Yadda yadda. Yadda, boy," Spooky says, which makes me think of Claudia, which makes me think of what just went down. Why did she play me like that?

"Uncle, can I ask you a question?"

"Uh-oh, this sounds heavy, Albert. I bet you it got something to do with that honeydew he had in here the other night," Spooky says, and then daps Clyfe. I look at Clyfe, 'cause this is the perfect time for him to throw in one of his senseless quotes that he's famous for.

"I got nusskins," he says. That's a first.

"Smalls, what do you want to know?"

"How do you know if you like a woman a lot or really love her, ya know what I'm sayin'?"

"Be specific," Spooky says.

"Yeah, Smalls, that's a loaded question, with two guns. Choose one. Like or love, son?"

"It's confusing, Unc. I thought we was kind of feeling each other, but we just had a little fight or something. I don't even know."

"Boy, by the way she was diving in your pool that night we walked in on y'all, I'd say she likes you," Spooky says, and starts laughing. "Mos' def."

"'How delicious is the winning of a first kiss at love's beginning.'" Clyfe finally says something that makes sense, even if I'm the only one who it means something to.

"Smalls, do you like this gal? A lot?"

"Well, I think."

"Again, be specific, boy. Which one is it?"

"I think about her a lot. I text her a lot. I mean, I think I like her."

"Boy, your nose is more open than the hole in a doughnut," Uncle Al hollers, and he and Spooky bowl over in laughter.

"Y'all are a big help," I tell them, but as loud as the three of them are laughing, they probably don't even hear me. I head up the stairs to the house.

"Smalls, the best way to find out if a woman loves you is to just ask her," Uncle Al yells after me. A car pulls up in front of the house.

"That's real talk," Spooky adds.

"Don't put off till tomorrow what you can ask today," Clyfe hollers, and I half ignore him as usual.

"Honeydew, Honeydew," I hear Spooky say. When I turn around, there is homegirl getting out of her car, with flowers. And a jumbo bag of sunflower seeds.

Claudia

"Those flowers for me, little lady?" I'm met on the front porch by Omar's uncle and two other guys. Omar's standing near the front door.

"Not exactly, Mr. Smalls, but next time, I got you. I promise."

"You were in such a big rush last time, ate all our good food and split. I didn't even get a chance to introduce you to these fine gentlemen. This here is Spooky, and the guy in the colorful suit is Clyfe." Colorful was an understatement. This guy looks like he could be a mascot for Crayola. Lavender suit, red shoes, and a purple-and-red hat. That's all kinds of wrong.

"Nice to meet you all." I shake Spooky's hand and think

they should call him Sweaty.

"If your heart is a volcano, how shall you expect flowers to bloom?" is what Clyfe asks when I shake his hand. So this is where Omar gets his random quotes from.

"What are you doing here, Claudia?" I'm on the bottom step; he's on the top looking down at me. His eyes are fire. Maybe the volcano is in his heart. At least he's talking to me.

"Boy, you ought to be ashamed of yourself," Spooky chides him.

"Smalls, talk to this woman like your momma raised you," Mr. Smalls adds.

"It's okay—he's just a little salty with me, and rightly so," I tell them.

"No excuse for being rude, not on my stoop," Mr. Smalls says.

"You old-timers let T-Diddy handle this." The three men look at each other, and then at him, and then at me, and then they laugh like somebody just told the best joke ever.

"Mr. Football thinks he's on the field," Mr. Smalls jokes. "This here is *my* stadium. I run this!"

"This boy is trying to quarterback us," Spooky says.

"Spooky, what was he just saying about love and wanting to know—"

"A'ight, a'ight, chill. Claudia, how you doing? Come on inside." He motions for me to follow him up the stairs.

"Yeah, that's what I thought, homeboy!" Mr. Smalls hollers. "Let us know if he starts tripping again, Claudia." I nod and smile, but not too much because Omar is looking at me with eyes ready to cut. "And don't be turning your music up so loud. Put your earphones on."

"Without music, life is a journey through a desert." I turn around, because that sounds way too familiar. Not the voice, but the words. I've read them before.

"Pat Conroy, right?" I ask Clyfe. He nods. "He's my favorite novelist."

"She's the first person on the planet to identify any of Clyfe's quotes. Methinks she's a keeper, boy," Spooky hollers after us.

When we get inside the house, I follow him into the living room. He sits down in a chair, which leaves me sitting on the couch by myself. Somewhere in the house, there is music playing. It's soft, but it grows louder with each second we sit in silence.

We're right across from each other, maybe two feet apart at the most. Feels like we're in a tunnel, on opposite ends.

"Oh, these are for you," I say, and set the vase of flowers

down on the coffee table that separates us.

"Roses, huh? These aren't my favorite."

"You don't have a favorite, Omar."

"What's my favorite color?"

"You don't have one."

"Wrong," he says confidently.

"You have two, orange and green."

"Well, whatever."

The silence takes over again. We look at everything but each other. He runs his finger along the seam of his jeans. I curl and uncurl my toes. He purses his lips. I smack mine. He rubs his ears. My phone rings. Jeez, I forgot to put it on vibrate.

"You need some privacy? I can step out while you talk to your little boyfriend, Leo."

I let the phone ring, even though it's probably my sister wondering where I am. We have a few more awkward minutes, and then I speak.

"You have any candles?"

"Random."

I get up, exploring his living room.

"What are you doing, Claudia Clarke?"

"Oh, now I'm Claudia Clarke. I prefer homegirl."

"Apparently, so do a lot of guys," he says, and gets up.

"Where do you keep your candles?"

"I don't know, maybe in the kitchen," he answers, and I walk into the kitchen and start rummaging through drawers. "Wow, this kitchen is immaculate. You not only cook, but you clean, too. I may just have to marry you." It comes out before I can catch myself. I turn around to see if he hears me, to see if maybe I just thought it and didn't say it. The quarter smirk on his face lets me know that, yep, I said it.

"There may be a big candle in the bathroom upstairs," he says, now half smiling.

"Perfect," I say. "Show me, but grab some matches first."

I follow him up the stairs. When we get to the top, he tells me, "Wait in the hallway." Then he walks into the bathroom. A few seconds later he comes back out with a deformed-looking candle and a book of matches. "Now what?"

"Take me to your room, Omar?" The smile on his face is gargantuan now. "In your dreams, homeboy."

"What is this, make-up sex? Are you trying to get back in my good graces?"

"Hardly. I just want to talk."

"Talk, huh? Yeah, right." He hands me the candle. "Okay, come on. You talk, I'll listen, Claudia Clarke." You're not going to make this easy for me, are you, Omar? He pulls out a key from his pocket and sticks it in the padlock that seals his room. A lock, really? Who does that?

His room is what I'd imagine a typical guy room looks like. As soon as we walk in, he starts picking up a ton of clothes off the floor and throwing them in the closet. Trophies line the shelves and windowsills. Newspapers, mainly the sports section, are strewed out all across the bed, which doesn't look like it's been made in decades. I know where I'm not sitting.

Sticking its head from underneath one of his pillows is a two-liter of Sprite. I guess he sees me eyeing it, because he tries to explain.

"I have to hide food and stuff, because of all the jokers coming through this place during the day. Got to protect my ish." That explains the padlock.

On the walls are framed black-and-white pictures of his family. While he's hiding junk—his version of cleaning—I look at the photos.

"Is this your mother? Wait a minute, Omar, this has got to be your dad; he's got your eyebrows. Where is your grandmother?"

"You sure do have a lot of questions. What are you, a reporter or something?" he says, and laughs out loud. "I'm done. So now what?" Still with the attitude.

"We're gonna play a game."

"What, like Scrabble in the dark? Jeopardy by candle-light? That's kind of wack, Claudia. This is your way of apologizing? I'm still pissed off."

"We're going to play the free game. My sister told me about it. It's real simple. But first I need you to turn off your cell phone, unplug all the clocks in the room, and take off your watch."

"What days do you have therapy?"

"Ha ha! Now sit down and cross your legs." He does, and I do the same, facing him. "And, the candle goes here." I place it in the middle and light the wick.

"Already this is loads of fun." I shoot him a mean look that says, Enough with the sarcasm.

"Patience, grasshopper. Now, hold my hands and look into my eyes."

"I've heard about this low-country Gullah voodoo stuff. You aren't trying to put a spell on T-Diddy, are you?" I grab his hands while the fire burns between us.

When he looks into my eyes, the fire shoots up, like a geyser of red and orange. Our eyes get wider, then the fire settles down. My sister told me that the energy between two bodies syncs with the fire from the candle, but I just took that as exaggeration. Maybe she was right.

"Okay, so here's how it goes. You ask me a question, and I have to answer it truthfully. Then I ask you a question, and you have to answer it truthfully," I say to him.

"Any question?"

"Yep, anything you want to know."

"And what if you lie?"

"If you lie, then you die. The other person has the right to set you on fire." I can feel his grip tighten. I start laughing profusely.

"Homegirl got jokes."

"Supposedly the more truth you share, the longer the fire burns. The longer the game goes on." The longer we're connected, Omar. "Plus we have to look in each other's eyes. It's hard to lie when you're looking dead at some one. You ready?"

"I'm going first."

"Fine, Omar. Go ahead."

"What did you and Leo do after I left?"

"I gave him some books that belonged to him, and he left."

"Did you kiss—"

"Wait a minute, it's my turn. Did you sleep with Kym King?"

"Uh, no. Did you kiss him?"

That was too quick. Don't think I'm not coming back to that question, mister. "Kiss him when?"

"You know when. Did you kiss Leo earlier tonight, after I left your place?"

"That would be no. You really ought to ask some better questions. What were you and your uncle talking about before I came up?" Judging by his hesitation, this is a good question. His grip tightens again.

"We were talking about a lot of things. The protest, and, uh, honeydew." He loosens his grip, but mine tightens.

"Honeydew fruit."

"Yeah, something like that." The fire wanes a little. "Here comes the big one, Claudia Clarke. You ready?"

"I'm ready, Omar."

"You ever kissed a girl?"

"That's what you wanted to know? You're making this way too easy, Omar. Yes, I have."

"Oh, snap, who?" and then he realizes it's my turn. "My bad."

"Why did you start the protest?" The fire shoots up between us. If I were into all that energy stuff, I'd say that this is a defining moment.

"I started the protest to, um, impress you—"

"And—"

"Hole up, hole up. I'm not finished. Be patient. And I was hoping that I could get you to think I was the kind of guy that you would go for. That you would, um, sleep with."

"Hmmm. Wow! That's pretty manipulative."

"That was then. I don't feel like that anymore. Have you been in West Charleston all your life?"

"I've been all over. I was born in California. Lived in Canada, which is where I learned French. Before we came to Charleston, we lived in Haiti, where my parents worked as missionaries. Where were you born?"

"I was born in New York, in St. Luke's Hospital. My mom's family is from Long Island, but my dad's family is from Beaufort. What do you think your parents would say about the protest?"

"I can tell you exactly what they would say, because I told them," I say proudly. "They are the ones who got me into social justice and peace. My mom told me, and I quote, 'Give 'em hell, Claudia. Make us proud.' And my dad said, 'Don't forget to take the car in for service.'" He laughs and does the curly-lip thing, and everything is on its way back to better. "Do you miss your mom and dad?"

"I miss my folks a lot. And Muppet."

"Muppet?" I mouth.

"Muppet is my basset hound back home. That's my dawg." Awwwwwwwww! "You think I can cook, but my mom is a beast in the kitchen. She used to make these things called pastalias. She'd wrap ground beef in home-made dough, brush it with butter, then bake. Best thing I ever ate. She taught me everything I know about cooking."

Hearing him talk about his mother like this reminds me why I'm feeling him. As if you need a reminder, Claudia. Jeez! He asks me about my mom and dad. I tell him they live in different third world countries half the year and here the other half. I find out his dad is an eye doctor who loves going to Broadway plays. I tell him Leo was a jerk, and that I hope I never see him again. He really opens up about play-ing football at Miami, and even though he's excited, he's nervous as hell. I tell him his secret is safe with me.

"When's your birthday, homegirl?" He called me homegirl again.

"Next week."

"Whoa! I didn't even know. That's what's up."

"When is yours?"

"August." He pauses like he's about to ask a deep ques-tion. "Don't think I forgot. Who was the girl you kissed?"

"And you were doing so well, Omar. I kissed two. My mother and my sister."

"Oh, you got me. I thought I was about to find out some juicy gossip. You know there's a rumor going on that your girl Blu is gay."

"That's not a rumor—she is," I say matter-of-factly. His head drops along with his jaw.

"Oh, snap! Wow!"

"It's not like she's hiding it. You got a problem with that?" I ask, and intentionally squeeze his hands tightly.

"No, no, actually it's kind of cool. So, you two ever—"

"What is it with guys' infatuation with two girls kissing? I never understood that!"

"Is that your question?" he asks me.

"No, my question is, 'Why me?'"

"OMG! Homegirl is getting deep now. Look at that fire, it's burning." He shifts. "How long we been in here? My butt's asleep."

"I feel you—I'm getting a little crick in my neck," I say, and stretch it from side to side.

"You want me to massage it for you?" he says, smiling that devilish smile he's perfected.

"First, you're holding my hand and you can't let go, because then the game is over. And second, answer the question, please."

"Why you? Hmmm. You, because throwing a ball is

nothing if you don't have someone to catch it." This makes me laugh. "You, because since I met you, I want to be better." This almost makes me tear. "You, Claudia Clarke, because before I met you, my world was as big as a football field. Now, it's an ocean." This makes me want to take off all my clothes and let him dive in. Again? Hurry up and ask me a question, Omar. Please. Before I do something stupid.

It's the staring that does it. My sister said that after playing the free game, you either fall madly in love or you never want to see each other again. It's that powerful. I can believe it. Keep it together, Claudia.

"Why'd you break up with college boy?" I so want to not be looking at him now. How can he ask me this question? There's the truth, and then there's part of the truth. I'm not gonna lie to him, but I'm not sharing that story. I'm not going into what went down like this, that's for sure.

"Why did y'all break up?"

"I heard you the first time," I say, a little testy. "We had a disagreement that got out of hand," I add warily. "He just wasn't the kind of man he pretended to be." For the first time in the game, the fire dies down a little, which makes me look even more suspicious. Before Omar challenges me, I jump in with my question.

"What does bong bong mean?"

"Oh, snap! No you didn't!" He starts laughing so hard, he almost falls to the side. "Really, homegirl?"

"Answer the question, please." At first I was just asking something to change the subject, but now I really want to know. "I'm waiting."

"It means, uh," he says, clearing his throat. "It means, uh, okay, first off, I didn't make this up, so don't be judging me and whatnot."

"Omar, just tell me. Jeez."

"It means banging on nasty girls."

"Is this what you tell people you're doing to me?"

"No!" he says emphatically. "Hole up, hole up. That was two questions. Is there a penalty or something for breaking the rules?"

"Not that I'm aware of."

"There is now. T-Diddy, I mean, I hereby institute a rule that says if you break any of the free game rules, you have to kiss the other person."

I shake my head.

"So far you owe me one kiss."

"Yeah, whatever, homeboy. Ask me your question." Actually, I owe him two kisses, but it is what it is.

My sister talks a lot about energy and karma and spirituality stuff. Just because Omar and I are holding hands and there's a candle burning, and the lights are out and our eyes are locked on each other, does not mean that our "energy" is connected. I've listened to my sister's spill time and time again, and I've always acted like I was interested in it. Primarily because she gets so amped up about it and because she's my sister. But the truth is I've never believed any of her mystical ideas. Until now. He says a bunch of stuff, but all I hear are the last five words.

"You ever have an abortion?" he asks.

OMAR

Homegirl thinks she's slick. I see the fire getting lower. That's kind of spooky, for real. But hey, maybe this game actually works. I'm going to call her on her lie, but just not now. She obviously doesn't want to talk about it. But don't think T-Diddy isn't keeping score. That's three, homegirl.

"Are you still mad at me?" she asks.

I'm a little salty, but I ain't really mad at her anymore. I mean, she did call him all kinds of jerks and whatnot. "Yep," I tell her, even though it's hard to keep the grin off my face.

I don't know how long we've been sitting here, but it feels like a forever. My butt is knocked out.

She asks me a question, then she slips up and asks me

another in the same breath. Let me lighten the mood a little.

"I hereby institute a rule that says if you break any of the free game rules, you have to kiss the other person." She shakes her head. "So far you owe me one kiss."

"Yeah, whatever, homeboy. Ask me your question."

Truth is, I don't really have any more questions. I've been watching her lips form words. Seeing her chest rise with each breath. Paying attention to each strand of black hair and the way it lies across her shoulder. I don't have any more questions, because I don't want to talk anymore. I know it sounds corny, but I want to pull her close to me and just be held. Be kissed. I just feel so good right now. Yeah, I want us to make some love, but not because of a hundred-and-fifty-dollar bet. I want to do it because I feel good with her. So good that I really don't want it to end.

I want her to know that I've been reading her blog, so I say, "I saw your article on teen pregnancy and abortion. I know several girls who've done it. You ever have an abortion?"

Her eyes get big. Her hands tighten around mine. Then they collapse. I see the perspiration forming on her forehead. Maybe it's the heat from the flame, because it's definitely not hot in here. By the way she drops her head to gaze at the candlelight, our eyes unglued for the first time in who knows how long, I know that something else is causing her to sweat.

"I'm sorry, Claudia, I shouldn't have asked that."

The tear that comes from her eye mixes with the sweat, and now I just want to hold her. I relax my hands, to wipe her tear, but she grabs me tighter.

"No, don't let go." Now she's crying even more. It's not like I've never had a girl crying in front of me. But this is different.

"It's just a game—we can stop. Let me get you a tissue, Claudia."

"No, I'm good," she says, and then tries to laugh but winds up crying some more. Something tells me to crack a joke, but something smarter tells me to just sit here and be quiet. And let her cry it out. Eventually she talks.

"I sort of lied a little when you asked me why Leo and I broke up," she admits, looking back up at me.

"Yeah, I caught that."

"What's that, like two kisses?"

"Actually, it's four now, but who's counting?" I squeeze her hand reassuringly, like my mother did me when I burned my first lemon pound cake.

"I was a virgin when I met Leo. I told you how religious

my parents are. Well, they didn't just forbid me and my sister to have sex, they actually told me if we did before we got married, we would die."

"Wow!"

"Yeah, exactly! So I grew up afraid of sex. I mean, what little girl wants to get murdered?" she adds, and offers a weak laugh. "My sister didn't buy any of it. When she became a Buddhist in college, she totally started having sex, not like a slut or anything, but she was like, 'If I'm in love, and the guy loves me, I'm going to share the temple of my body with him.'"

"Whoa!" The temple of my body.

"I know, right. I'm not sure what being a Buddhist had to do with it, but she definitely was a free spirit. My parents hated it, but she was in college, so they really couldn't do anything about it. Anyway, a few years ago, I went to a party with her, and I met Leo. He was a college freshman." She pauses, looks at me even more intently than she's been doing all night. It's almost as if she's deciding if she should go on or not. I got you, homegirl.

"I got an itch," I say. "I need to scratch my head." I pull her hand on top of my head, and we both rub together. "Oh, that feels so much better. Thanks. Okay, continue." She gives me a half smile.

"Fast forward a year, and Leo and I are getting serious. He's telling me he loves me, talking about marrying me one day. I'm happier than I've been. But I still haven't had sex with him."

"Because of the whole being-killed thing," I say, and she laughs out loud, which is a relief, because I know this is tough for her to talk about. Whatever this is.

"Right. So, one day, I'm at his dorm room studying. He's working on a song. Did I tell you he plays guitar?" I shake my head. "Well, yeah, he plays neo-soul. Anyway, so he tells me to listen to something he wrote. And he plays this incredible song about me and how I'm the apple of his eye and he wants to peel me, and it's just this beautiful, touching song. Well, at least I thought it was then, but in actuality it was just a song he sang to impress me, to get me into bed. Sound familiar?" Now I feel really stupid.

"Did it work?"

"You already asked your question, friend. Now you owe me."

"I'll be glad to pay my debt."

"I bet you would. Anyway, after hearing this remarkable love song, I kiss him. I end up spending the night, and sharing the 'temple of my body' with him. And apparently my parents were lying, because I didn't die." The fire is blazing higher and brighter than it has since the beginning of this game.

"Afterward, he changes. I mean he literally changes the next morning. He doesn't call me every day like he did before; has meetings all of a sudden and can only see me on Tuesdays. This goes on for a month or so. One day I show up on a Wednesday, because I miss him." She pauses and squeezes my hand hard. "Actually, not just because I missed him, but because I had to tell him something important."

"And he's with another chick." I knew he was cheating on her.

"Well, yeah, but as it turns out, he was with several other chicks. Playa had a different one every night." All of a sudden, the word "playa" doesn't sound so cool anymore. "I cried all the way home and into the next morning. I don't think I even went to school the next day. What I'd wanted to tell him was that my period was late."

This hits me like a sledgehammer. Knocks me so hard I almost fall backward. I hold her hands tighter to keep my balance.

"He's avoiding me, but one day I catch him as he's leaving work, at a clothing store on King Street. He hugs me, tries to act like he's been so busy, but he's happy to see me.

I tell him I think he's going to be a father. I don't know why I said 'I think,' because by then I was almost two months late and three tests had been positive. He doesn't even pause to think or smile or frown. He just looks at me all nonchalantly and says, 'Maybe it's not mine.' Like I wasn't a virgin before him. Like there was another guy, other guys, that I'd been with. Like I was just some rotten apple that he'd thrown away.

"He came over later and apologized, and I thought that maybe I had misjudged him, that maybe it was me, not him. And then he kissed me on the cheek, slapped four hundred-dollar bills on the table, and turned to leave. 'It was just bad luck, Claudia,' he said. "I mean, we did use protection. How the hell unlucky is it that the condom broke?' and then he laughs, like it's a big joke. 'Look, I'm heading out of town for the weekend, so I won't be able to take you to get the procedure done. I'm sure you'll figure it out, though. I'll holla.'

"He called it a procedure. Like lying back with my legs spread wide, altering destiny for all of eternity, is a fucking procedure. Sure, I asked him if he had protection, but why didn't I ask him if he had enough of it to guard my heart, to give shelter to my soul in case of emergency?

"My sister took me to the clinic, sat with me while I

waited to be called. Held me when I came out bawling. Told me everything was going to be all right. Took me home, put me to bed, watched over me. I never thought I would be one of those girls. It was the worst day of my life. And I've never talked about it with anyone, not even Blu. I just felt so stupid and horrible." She takes my hand, and we wipe the tears that are coming fast and furious. "So to answer your question—"

"Finally," I say, hoping that my attempt at sarcasm will make her smile, even a little. It does.

"Yes, I had an abortion." We are both hushed. We sit quietly, staring at each other, listening to our hearts beat. I want to tell her I'm sorry. There are simply no words to punctuate the air. I am sorry.

After about ten minutes, she finally says, "Thank you, Omar."

"For what?" I ask.

"For letting me open up with you. Now don't you start tearing up, too," she says.

"Ain't nobody crying over here," I say, sniffling.

I wish homegirl didn't have to go through that mess. Ol' dude really is a jerk. Am I? I know a couple of girls who had abortions. I even went with one of my exes in Brooklyn, to get one. It wasn't a big deal. Until today.

226

"Liar! That's two kisses you owe me," she says, trying to lighten the mood.

"You all right, Claudia?"

It feels like an hour of quiet passes between us. Thing is, it's not even awkward. I feel close enough that I can smell her mint breath. I would have said something by now, but I don't know what to say. Give me a football and eleven guys bulldozing toward me, and I can figure out what to do in a split second. But this situation is strange and unfamiliar. So I sit here, tightly clutching her hands, waiting for Claudia. To. Be. Okay.

"Enough of the drama. This is supposed to be a fun game," she says, as if she can hear my thoughts.

"You okay?"

"Uh, you already asked that question. Yes. My turn. Omar Smalls, are you afraid of death?"

"Wow, really. Yeah, this is a lot of fun now," I say, and we both laugh. "I don't know, I've never thought about it. I don't want to die. I got a lot of things I want to do."

"Like what?"

"Like play in the NFL. Like buy my uncle Al a pimped-out RV, so he can hit the road with his boys. Like travel. Like get the arts funding back. I've been thinking about it, and we should have better textbooks. And we should have a school marching band. And we should be a better school. Feel me."

"Omar Smalls wants to change the world. Go figure!"

"I also want to be your dude, like really."

"I feel you, babe." She calls me babe about fifteen more times during the game, and it sounds better than any nickname I've ever had. Even T-Diddy. We ask each other questions about random stuff, like favorite TV shows and rappers. We talk about girls I've dated. She tells me about the time she cheated on a spelling test in fifth grade. I tell her about how I'd like to have my own cooking show one day. After my NFL career, of course.

The free game goes on and on, until the light from the candle is no longer our source of illumination. Until we look out the window and see a remarkable sight.

The sun.

Claudia

After I take a shower, I throw on one of Omar's hooded Miami sweatshirts and a pair of jeans I have in the trunk. There are no extra toothbrushes in the house, at least ones that are unused, so I use my finger. No lotion either, so my face is close to ashy. Not a good look, Claudia.

Fortunately, Mr. Smalls is a late sleeper, because I'd hate for him to get the wrong idea about me.

"Thanks for getting my jeans. Is it cold out there?' I ask him.

"Colder than a witches's nose," he says, laughing.

"Did you call your sister?"

"I left her a note to let her know where I was going last night. Trust me, she's not the worrying type." One of the perks of having a free-spirit older sister and parents gone for half the year. "Plus my phone's dead. Forgot to plug it up last night."

"Yeah, mine too."

Omar checks the hallway first and then motions for me to come. He holds my hand as we tiptoe down the stairs and out the door.

"I thought y'all didn't have cold winters down here. Sure feels like winter. I've got to run back in the house—T-Diddy needs a hat." He lets my hand go, and now I feel even colder.

In the car, I look at the dashboard and it reads twenty-nine degrees. I put the hood over my head and blast the heat. When Omar gets in, he leans over and kisses me on the cheek.

"Why'd you do that?" I ask.

"The free game is over, enough with the questions, homegirl. Just drive." And like it's the most normal thing, he sticks his left hand under my right thigh and leaves it there. "I need some hot chocolate. Can we make a run to Starbucks or something?"

"Oh, shizzle! I was supposed to pick up Blu for coffee this morning."

"Shizzle, really?" He shakes his head and laughs.

"I'm serious. Blu and I go for coffee every Tuesday and Thursday. We've been doing it for years."

"She'll understand. Just tell her you're in love."

"So I should lie to her." Now it's my time to laugh.

"Whatever." He moves his hand from under my leg like his feelings are hurt.

"It's not love, Omar. It's just a lot of like. It takes time to love someone."

"Well, then give me some of that like." He leans over to kiss me on the cheek again.

"Omar, you don't learn to love someone in sixteen days."

"You've been counting, huh? Sixteen days or sixteen years, it's all the same. All I know is in this cold, harsh world, you are my winter coat."

"Who said that, Omar?"

"That's all me, homegirl. Give me some time, Claudia Clarke, and I could learn to love you completely. Now let's go to Starbucks. What's up with the heat in this car?"

The line at Starbucks is so frickin' long that we decide to skip it and just grab some of the watered-down hot chocolate and muffins in the school cafeteria.

The TV cameras are still in front of our school. Fortunately, we can park around back and go in through the gym, which Omar has the code to. One of the perks of being Mr. Football.

"Sixty-five minutes is like the whole first period. I feel kind of bad for Mr. Washington."

"Why? He's riding with us."

"True. I hope you don't get suspended again. Actually, I hope you don't get expelled this time."

"She's not going to suspend me again. Uncle Al's lawyer sent her an email about freedom of speech and whatnot. Nobody gonna break my stride."

Omar tries to hold my hand in the hallway, but I pull it away. He tries again, and I do it again. Not because I don't want him to hold my hand; it's just that my emotions are still a roller coaster. I tell myself if he just does it one more time, grabs my hand, I will let him. He does.

Hand in hand, we walk into the noisy cafeteria, where every student who gets to school early hangs out. Some people eat, some don't. But almost everybody has a jumbo cup of iced tea.

The cooks at our school make the best sweet tea on earth, but they haven't quite figured out that hot chocolate requires more than a teaspoon of chocolate powder in an eight-ounce cup of hot water. Jeez!

Once we're inside, and a few people see us, I wonder what the response is going to be. Not for Omar, because people are used to seeing him with any and every girl. But no one, except Blu, has ever seen me with a guy. And I've never dated a guy at West Charleston. This should be interesting.

We walk past a few students, and they stand up, face us, and start clapping. A few more do the same. It's like the domino effect. Before you know it, the entire cafeteria, even the cooks, are applauding us. I'm thinking, Are they joking us, or are they seriously that happy we're together?

A few minutes ago, when we were on the other side of the cafeteria door, I didn't know what to expect. Sure wasn't this spectacle. Even the cafeteria workers are clapping. It's like we're the president and Michelle.

Omar, of course, eats it up. He starts waving at folks like he's the frickin' president.

"Omar, what's going on?"

"I don't know, homegirl, but it's kind of cool, right?"

Luther, the smoker kid, jumps up on a table.

"Attention, attention!" He stomps his big black boots, and everyone turns to face him.

"When we started the silent treatment, we didn't know what we were doing. Some of us even thought being silent was silly. Real talk." More applause. "We didn't know if it would work. We just took Omar and Claudia's word for it." Are we getting some kind of award?

"We trusted them to right the wrongs at West Charleston. We trusted them to lead us to the promised land."

Loud chants begin to race through the cafeteria. "WE'RE FIRED UP, CAN'T TAKE NO MO'! WE'RE FIRED UP, CAN'T TAKE NO MO'!"

"Today, we shout out Omar and Claudia," Luther continues, "for keeping it real, for representing West Charleston, for getting the band and the drama club reinstated. YEAH!" Omar and I look at each other, unsure of whether we're dreaming. We've just spent the last ten hours sitting on opposite sides of a lit candle and staring into each other's eyes. Surely we could be asleep and this could all be a dream. "It worked?" I mumble to him.

"T-Diddy, you're the man. Thanks, dawg, we're going to the Battle of the Bands. That's what's up," Belafonte comes over and says.

"T-DiddyAndBeyoncéRunThisWorld," Freddie says, and winks at T-Diddy.

"I guess we did it, homegirl. Yeah, it worked. Wow!" My

head is spinning. The last time I was this happy was when my dad took me to meet Alice Walker, my other favorite writer, and she invited us to have dinner with her.

I see Blu walking toward me. Finally someone's going to congratulate me for the work that I did.

"Trick, you nixed me for some jock. Really?" she says, laughing. I slide my hand out of Omar's, and he kind of looks at me like, "What's up?" Blu and I head over to get some hot chocolate.

"My bad, Blu, time got away from me," I say, trying not to blush.

"Yeah, I bet. Nice shirt." And she rolls her eyes.

"So we got the dance team back. That's great."

"Don't try to change the subject. Did he smash?"

"Nope, we just played a game that lasted all night," which is technically true.

"Your nose is growing, trick." Even though she is my best friend, I'm just not ready to tell her about Folly Beach. But I will. "You didn't check your email?"

"My phone is dead."

"Girl, the school board held a special meeting last night. They gave us the band back and a few other things."

"Thank the lord," I say.

"Don't go hallelujahing already."

"What?"

"The library is still closed. And the school board said they may have to make another round of layoffs."

Before I can react to this nonsense, someone pushes me in the back.

"You're fired, bish," Kym King says from behind me. "You think you're all that. I got something for you. Believe that."

"I got something for you too," I say, feeling a little cocky and over-the-top happy. "A breath mint." Blu laughs.

"What you laughing at, dude?" Kym says, emphasizing the last word.

"Don't let that trick walk in here all disrespectful, holding your Omar's hand, and then try to play you," Eve says, instigating.

"Yeah, don't do that," Blu says, then reaches into her purse. She pulls out a small container of Vaseline and then starts rubbing it all over her face. "If we're going to blows, let's do this, then. This *dude* is ready to rumble."

We all stare at each other for like two minutes, in silence. It's kind of ironic how we've all become pros at this quiet thing.

"Let's go, Eve. You had your chance, Claudia. I tried to warn your little stupid tail. Now it's on." She and Eve leave.

"Dayum, I was looking forward to whooping her ass. She's been asking for it since fifth grade," Blu says.

"What are you going to do with all that Vaseline, Blu?"

"Oh, that's easy. Come here." And she starts wiping my hands on her face. "Apparently Omar didn't have any lotion at his place, Ashy." And I don't even try to hide the huge smile on my face.

OMAR

"Today, we're sitting down with South Carolina's Mr. Football, who also happens to be the brainchild behind the recent silent protest at West Charleston High School. Omar 'T-Diddy' Smalls, thank you for joining us on CNN's *Evening Edition*."

"Thank you for having me. But if I can first say one thing, it wasn't just my brainchild. My homegirl Claudia Clarke and all the students at West Charleston High School made the silent treatment happen." I look directly at the camera, even though they told me not to, and add, "Go, Panthers!"

"Generally we don't normally think of high school students as being interested in political activities. So how did this all come about?"

"Anderson, it's because of those kinds of perceptions that teenagers don't care. The time is over where teenagers will take whatever, that we will accept being classified as uncaring. The students at West Charleston High School have decided that we are fired up, and we won't take no more."

"Yes, I know that was one of your rallying calls. Did you come up with that?"

"I'm from Brooklyn originally, but I came down here to live with my uncle Al, who runs the Library of Progress."

"Great name. Library of Progress."

"Yeah, it's a community center that offers programs for people in West Charleston. Anyway, Uncle Al and some of his buddies were schooling me on all the protests and revolutions that they were involved in during the sixties and seventies."

"Before you were born."

"Way before T-Diddy Smalls was born. So I really got to shout out to the fellas at the Library of Progress: Uncle Al, Clyfe, and Spooky." I smile at the camera again and throw up the peace sign. It's ten minutes into the interview and I'm killing it.

"Al, he said my name, he said my name on national TV," Spooky hollers, and we bust out laughing. "I got to go call my momma. I'm famous."

"Heck, we're all famous. Smalls shouted us all out. See that suit he's wearing? His daddy sent me the money for it. Smalls, tell these jokers who picked that suit out for you."

"I'm just glad you didn't let Clyfe pick it out," Spooky says, and we all laugh some more.

"C'mon son, T-Diddy's on CNN. This is my big debut, can y'all let me finish the interview."

"Smalls, you're lucky Honeydew is here, because I don't like being told what to do." He unmutes the TV.

"See, now y'all done missed most of the interview, this is the end."

"That was a quick debut, boy," Spooky says.

"Smalls is probably going to watch it ten more times tonight anyway."

"Shhhhhh! Here it comes," I tell him.

"I'm sure a lot of our viewers want to know where the nickname T-Diddy came from," Anderson asks.

"My teammates call me T-Diddy. It started in Pop Warner, when I scored five touchdowns in one game—two on offense, three on defense—and my coach started calling me Touchdown. Then in middle school, it got shortened to TD. When I moved to Charleston, I remixed it, Bad Boy style. Now I'm T-Diddy."

"Can't nobody hold you down," he raps.

"Hole up, hole up, let me find out Anderson Cooper is onto that hip-hop."

"Who doesn't like Jay-Z?" he says, and then gives me a pound. This woadie is hilarious. "Well, T-Diddy, congratulations on the important work that you're doing at West Charleston. And kudos to you for standing up against the arts funding cuts in your school, a tragedy happening in districts across the country."

"Well, it's not over. We still have more work to do."

"So the protest is not over?"

"Well, the silent protest is over for now, but I think our eyes have been opened to what's possible. We started a job, and we won't stop, can't stop, until we finish. I think it was Dr. King who said, 'Freedom is never voluntarily given by the oppressor; it must be demanded by the oppressed.'"

"Quoting Sean 'Diddy' Combs and Martin Luther King in the same breath. There you have it, folks. A true hip-hop activist. Well said, Mr. Smalls—or should I call you T-Diddy?"

"It doesn't matter what you call me, Anderson, it's who I answer to."

"That boy straight stole Clyfe's words. Clyfe, you

believe that," Spooky interjects.

"Imitation is the sincerest flattery," Clyfe says in true fashion.

"Just one more thing, Omar," Anderson says. "I hear that you're headed to play college football next year, and I'm sure that a lot of gamecocks would be happy if you chose USC. And as a proud alumnus of Yale, I must put in a plug for the Bulldogs."

"South Carolina was definitely one of my top schools. This state has been real good to me."

"I understand, Omar, that you haven't formally made your announcement due to some, uh, extenuating circumstances."

"That is correct."

"Well, would you like to announce your decision here on CNN?" Heck yeah. I look dead at the camera.

"To all my fans, to my supporters, to all of the students at West Charleston High School. To homegirl for showing me how to swim, to Luther, Belafonte, and Blu for getting down with the movement, to Fast Freddie, Willie Mack, and the rest of my teammates; to Coach, but especially to my family—Uncle Al, Mom, Dad, thank you for your support and guidance." I take the cap off my lap, place it on my head so the viewers can see the big orange-and-green U.

"I've decided to take my talents to South Beach."

"You heard it here first, folks. Breaking news on CNN: the country's number-one star recruit, Omar 'T-Diddy' Smalls, has signed a letter of intent with the University of Miami."

"This boy thinks he's LeBron James now," Spooky chides.

Claudia, who is now leaning on my shoulder, hasn't said a whole lot. When I look at her, she's drooling slightly and fast asleep. I put a pillow on my lap and lay her head on it. She kicks her feet up on the sofa, and Spooky drapes a blanket over her.

"Smalls, I hope you ain't running no game on her. Little lady is not like all them other girls you run with," Uncle Al says to me.

"What're your intentions with Honeydew?" Spooky asks.

"Intentions? C'mon, son, I got this. Unc, pass my cell phone, I need to call Mom and Pops." They're acting like she's their daughter or something.

"I'm just saying, don't mess around and mess this up. She's a special one," Uncle Al says.

"We are not special. We are not crap or trash, either. We just are. We just are, and what happens just happens."

"Yeah, what Clyfe says," Spooky says, giving him the side eye. "Anybody want more lobster macaroni and cheese? If football doesn't work out, boy, you need to be all up in the Olive Gardens. Al, he put a hurtin' on that dish."

"Yeah, little lady needs to come around more often," Uncle Al hollers after him, implying that I only cook like this when Claudia comes over. He's right.

I make turkey chili the next night. On Friday, I make BBQ chicken, sweet potatoes, and wild rice. Usually Spooky and Clyfe have gone by the time we eat dinner. But not this week. And usually there are leftovers. Again, not this week. Each night, these jokers eat two and three helpings, like they haven't eaten all month.

"Boy, I didn't eat all day, hoping you were cooking up some magic," Spooky says with a mustache covered in BBQ sauce. "That was some good eats." He sets his plate down on the counter.

"What did you think about the wild rice? I made that," Claudia, my sous-chef, says.

"Best part of the meal," Uncle Al says as he puts a last spoonful in his mouth.

"Yeah, she got the recipe from her Uncle Ben," I say, and she punches me in the stomach. I grab her around the waist and pick her up and put her on the counter next to the dishes we're washing.

"Hey, get a room," Spooky says.

"None of that," Uncle Al adds. "I run a respectable center. Don't make me call Clyfe in here to wax poetic." Claudia kisses me on the forehead and we resume cleaning the dishes.

"Why doesn't your uncle have a dishwasher?"

"Same reason I don't have a microwave. People need to stop trying to find shortcuts to living. It's not always about doing the easy thing," Uncle Al lectures.

"Now you've done it," I say to Claudia.

Uncle Al continues. "When I was your age, we didn't even have water in the house. When it was time to take a bath, winter or summer, we had to run out to the well—"

"See! I hope you're ready for a sermon, little lady," I say.

Claudia and I spend the next three days together, hanging out some nights way past midnight.

I've never cried after seeing a movie, but on Saturday, when she takes me to see *The Visitor*, about a dude who gets jailed, deported, and taken away from his wife, I try to fight back the tears.

"You okay, Omar?" Claudia asks.

"Yeah, I'm good," I say, still fighting. When I was in fifth grade, there was this Puerto Rican girl named Lisa who lived around my way. We used to ride bikes, play handball, and sometimes she would stay over my house when her mom had to work late.

We'd wait for my parents to fall asleep, then we'd sneak into the basement and listen to my dad's records. Stuff like Al Green and Sam Cooke. I guess we found the music funny, 'cause we laughed a lot.

Eventually we would get to the reason we came down there in the first place. Spin the bottle. Lisa was the first girl I kissed. I thought about her all the time, and even cried a few times when she'd go out of town, like during the summers.

First day of sixth grade, I was walking to the bus stop, with a note that I'd written for her, confessing my love. I couldn't wait to see her. Maybe kiss her in the back of the bus.

Imagine my surprise when I got to the bus, and she wasn't there. After school, I went looking for her at her apartment building. Her neighbors told me that she was gone. Her family had moved back to Puerto Rico. I cried the whole way home. Lisa was the only girl I'd ever almost told 'I love you.' Until today.

"What's on your mind, babe?"

"I think I, uh, Claudia, I'm kinda . . ."

"Yeah, I know, Omar. Me too," she says, like the words are written all over my face.

And then we just hold each other, long after the credits have ended. If any of my teammates had seen me, it'd be over.

To celebrate Claudia's full scholarship, I plan a catfish fry. A bunch of my friends, and Blu, show up. I try to get Uncle Al to put on some Kanye or Common, but he chooses some jazz. It's a'ight, but it's not party music.

"Surprise!" Belafonte and Fast Freddie yell as Claudia walks through the door.

"C'mon son, this ain't no surprise party, we just celebrating homegirl getting a full ride to Harvard," I tell them.

"Wow, you did all this for me?" Claudia says sarcastically.

"Trick, come on, I'm starving, and Mr. Football wouldn't let us eat till you got here," Blu says, already sitting at the head of table.

"My bad, babe," Claudia says, kissing me on the lips. "I was Skyping with my parents to tell them the great news. But I'm here now—break out the bubbly."

"No bubbly in my house," Uncle Al says, wheeling his

chair in the living room. "Smalls, bring out the sparkling apple cider."

"AwwwC'monUncleAlYouTryingToRuinThisHouse-Party?" Fast Freddie jokes.

"Yeah, what's that noise we're listening to?" Willie Mack jokes.

"My house, my music, my rules. And why is that boy always talking like a locomotive? Slow down, Conductor Boy!"

"What's the problem? This music is dope. Uncle Al, what is it?" Claudia asks.

"Real music. Something the rest of these jokers don't have a clue about. This here is 'Ruby, My Dear.'"

"Thelonius Monk," she says confidently. Uncle Al starts spinning around in his wheelchair and rolls out to the front porch.

"Hey, Spooky, Harvard got culture too. She's on to that bebop. Little lady is world class." I look at her, and she just shrugs.

"What can I say—Claudia Clarke has got it going on," she says. Third person, really.

"T, what are we waiting on? She's here. Let's grub," Willie Mack says.

"Dinner is served," I holler, and the fifty-eleven people

in the house scurry to the table. Belafonte is the only one of us who goes to church regularly, mainly because he plays drums in the choir. "B, can you grace the table?" I turn off the music.

"Lord, today we come before you to ask that you nourish our hungry bodies with this food. We ask that you seriously protect us from the hands that prepared it. SERIOUSLY.

"We thank you for bringing us all together today, even Luther Lee and his girlfriend, who both smell like a tobacco factory, no offense. Lord, today we send a special shout-out to the folks at Harvard for taking this poor dance-challenged soul off our hands. West Charleston will be better for it.

"We ask that you allow the Panther marching band to win the Battle of the Bands. We know that other bands are worthy, but we ask that you allow them to win maybe another year, but not this one. I sure hope you're listening.

"And finally, Lord, we say a special thanks to Claudia for occupying T-Diddy's time. Since they hooked up—"

"C'mon son."

"Since they hooked up, he doesn't come around much anymore. It's like he doesn't know his boys anymore. The good thing is, at least we haven't been forced to watch the state championship football game another time. Please, we beg you, no mo'."

"Amen," Willie Mack echoes. "Amen to that."

"Uncle Al, y'all come on and eat," I scream out to the porch. "Grab the remote for me," I add, and snub my nose at the jokers chowing down on T-Diddy's famous gumbo and Cajun catfish.

Claudia

Save the Light

by Claudia Clarke

This Saturday, come on out to the Festival of Folly. There will be an oyster roast, a 3K walk/run, a seaside tour of gorgeous Folly Beach homes, and children's activities. The festival is a fundraiser for the Save the Light foundation, a nonprofit that raises funds to restore and prevent the lighthouse (located near Charleston and Folly Beach) from being lost to the sea. Click here for background and history of the lighthouse.

The festival will also feature free fishing, prizes, and a special parade featuring the newly reinstated

West Charleston High School Marching Panthers Band. "Don't call it a comeback—we been here for years," says Belafonte Jones, the drum major for the Panthers marching band. "Even though they eliminated the band, some of us still practiced, and we got a show for y'all. Believe that." This will be the first performance by the West Charleston marching band since it was shut down by the West Charleston school board more than twelve days ago.

Save the Light would like to convey a big thank-you to the WCHS students, the Folly Beach community, and visitors for their support during this historic preservation process. For more information and tickets, visit Save the Light's website.

Arrested Rappers Get Record Deal

by Blu McCants

In a strange turn of events, two rappers turned bank robbers pleaded guilty to all charges and then announced that they'd been offered a record deal with Green Mile Records. "Yeah yeah, Redbone and Hoe Daddy representing the eight-four-three," Redbone said outside the courthouse after their arraignment. "Me and Hoe Daddy going into the studio as soon as we get in."

The South Carolina state prison has recently installed mobile recording studios to accommodate all the young black men who are enrolling.

"Only in the country, girl. You couldn't make this stuff up," Blu says.

"I know, right. Straight comedy! Hurry up and finish, so I can post this and meet Omar."

"Why you rushing me, trick? Omar ain't thinking about you."

"Wrong. I'm all Omar is thinking about."

Mr. Football Heads to South Beach
by Blu McCants

Omar Smalls, South Carolina's Mr. Football, recently made an appearance on CNN's *Evening Edition*, where he announced what most of us at West Charleston already knew: he'll be playing football at the University of Miami next year. "I'll be representing West Charleston and Brooklyn, believe that. It's a dream come true," he said in an email. To find out about Omar Smalls's plans and the one thing he loves more than football, <u>click here for a full profile</u>.

Student Protest Yields Results

by Claudia Clarke

After twelve days of the "silent protest," school officials announced on January 26 that some of the students' demands would be met. In a morning announcement, and on the school Facebook page, Dr. Jackson informed the student body that the band, drama, and visual arts programs would be reinstated. Originally cut to make a dent in the school district's severe budget deficit, the programs "are vital to the morale and academic achievement of our students," she said.

Called the silent treatment, the nonviolent protest was supported by students, teachers, and national media alike. As word got around of the protest, schools across the state began their own silent protests. Even a few celebrities sent words of encouragement. Charleston's own, country singer Darius Rucker, showed solidarity for the students with a special song at one of his concerts last weekend in Columbia. During a recent episode of his Comedy Central show, even Stephen Colbert, another native Charlestonian, voiced his concern. Colbert, who funded a new arts award at the University of Virginia, was interviewing the actor Bill Murray about his latest movie and the minor-league baseball team he owns in Charleston when Murray mentioned the protest.

Luther Lee, a senior and staunch supporter of the silent treatment, had this to say: "I hope everyone learned something from this. We didn't have to raise our fists. We didn't have to fuss and fight. We used our silence to fight. We fought together, and we won."

While we certainly proved something major with our concerted effort, this fight is far from over. Several of our teachers are still without full-time jobs and thus health insurance. Next Monday, the school board will meet to decide their fate. While we wait for the verdict, let us remember that if we've learned anything during this protest, it's that we are a family. And families stick together. We have every hope that the school board will do the right thing. We won't be quiet if they don't!

OMAR

When she gets home from school today, there will be a plain brown envelope. It will contain a CD. Written on it in black Sharpie will be PLAY ME.

When she puts it in her laptop, it will play the *Mission: Impossible* song, and then my voice will come on: "Your mission, should you choose to accept it, is to make your way to the middle of Marion Square, at *exactly* five twenty-seven p.m. Eastern Standard Time. There you will rendezvous with a stunningly attractive dude who will be wearing a suit and holding indigo tulips. He will also have on orange-and-green underwear. The future of the free world is now in your hands. This CD will self-destruct in five seconds."

* * *

256

"You're early."

"I was excited. I thought maybe I had a secret admirer or something. But I see it's just you."

"Oh, you got jokes, do you?" I say to Claudia, and grab her hand. "Walk with me, birthday girl."

"Where are my tulips?"

"Tulips. Plural, really? Why not just tulip? Let me find out Claudia Clarke is high maintenance."

"Uh, you're the one who said I was getting tulips. I'm just saying."

"I changed my mind. Come on, let's walk."

I put my arms around her and we walk to the corner of King and Calhoun. There's a skinny little black boy in a hooded black shirt selling sweetgrass flowers. He head-nods me and comes up. Normally I walk by, never even look these jokers in the eye. I just pretend they don't even exist.

"What's good?" I ask him. He looks at the basket of flowers on the ground next to him.

"Dem flowers fuh sell," he says to us, in Gullah accent.

"How many you got, homeboy?"

"Mo' nuh da," he says. *I have no idea.* The kid puts two dirty pinky fingers in his mouth and whistles loud as a train. Seconds later, about three more boys with baskets rush over.

"I need a double deuce," I say, flashing two fingers twice.

He whispers to the group, and they weave twenty-two sweetgrass flowers right there on the spot. "How long?"

"Fas'," he says, not looking up.

"Cool, how much?"

"T'ree."

"C'mon son, three dollars?" I say to this little hustler. Claudia bows me in the ribs. "What, he's trying to get over on a brother," I say, smiling at her. "Look, I'll give you two dollars each, homeboy."

"Two and haff," he counters immediately.

"Little man, you ought to move to New York, 'cause you keepin' it really hood. That's cool, though. Holla at us when you finish, we'll be over there," I say, pointing to a nearby bench.

"Omar, you still trying to impress me, I see."

"It ain't even like that. I was going to get tulips for your birthday, 'cause you know that's your favorite flower and all," I say, smiling. "But I figured that these kids could probably use the money more than them big flower shops."

"Awww, that is so sweet!" She kisses me on the lips and makes a soft, moaning, sexy sound. "But why twenty-two?"

"I'm surprised you don't know, homegirl. Today is our

twenty-two-day anniversary from when we met at the house party. For each day that I've gotten to know you a little better. For each day that we've grown closer. For each day that I've realized that there is no other girl on earth who rocks my world like you do. For each day that we've changed the world together, I am getting one flower." I get down on one knee, like I'm about to propose. I'm not, LOL. She starts getting all teary-eyed.

"The sweetgrass plant was originally harvested by slaves in South Carolina. It's now considered a treasure. Claudia Clarke, you have harvested me from a boy to a man." I don't even care how corny it sounds. I'm feeling it. Feeling her. "Happy birthday, homegirl." And I hand her a gift.

"Wow, I don't know what to say, Omar." She kisses me on my cheek. "But a book? Really, for my birthday. No jewelry or cash even," she adds, chuckling.

"Maybe you should just open it, homegirl."

She does. Slowly. Carefully peeling back each corner of tape, slowly pulling the wrapping off. Yes, it is a book, homegirl, but not just any old book. How do girls cry and laugh at the same time? Never understood that.

"My bad—you don't like it," I say sarcastically.

"No, it's not that. It's just that, uh, you remembered.

He's my favorite," she says, thumbing through the book. *The Pat Conroy Cookbook.* Yeah! I wipe her tears with my finger. "Omar, why is there a stain on this page?"

"Oh, you know I had to try out the shrimp and grits recipe. That joint was fire! Pat Conroy is the best chef I ever read."

She gives me a look. "He's not a chef, Omar."

"I know, homegirl. Just messing with you. I picked up one of his novels at the library last week. A little long, but he's a decent writer."

"Omar, I'm a decent writer. Pat Conroy is the best frickin' novelist ever."

"Happy birthday, beautiful. I hope you enjoy it."

"I love it, Omar, and I love—"

"Heh." The boy in the hoodie interrupts, handing me the sweetgrass flowers. I give him two twenties and a ten and tell him to keep the change.

"Appreciate that, homeboy. Be easy," and then I hand the flowers to Claudia. "Happy birthday, beautiful," I say, and give her the T-Diddy special kiss, with my hand cradling the back of her neck. Oh yeah!

"Omar Smalls, you do rock my world." She stands up, leans into me, and we kiss again in the middle of Marion Square like we own the night.

"Homegirl, plenty of time for this, but we gots to be out. We're on a schedule."

"Out? We are out. Where else are we going?" I pinch my lips together with my fingers. "Everything's a big secret tonight, huh, Tom Cruise? Okay, I'll play along. Just as long as you don't try to blindfold me."

"Well, actually . . . ," I say, and pull out an orange-and-green bandanna. She almost has a conniption.

"You're insane. I'm not putting that on."

"Trust me, Claudia. I got you. You'll be happy, I promise." I spin her around and place the bandanna over her eyes and around her head.

"Please don't mess up my hair, I just got it done. Jeez."

I tie it, but not too tight, and then grab her hand. "Okay, just stay close to me—I got you. Let's walk."

We cross the street, just to throw her off a little. I take her back down King Street. We pass the Frances Marion Hotel, St. John's Lutheran church, and a doctor's office. When we get to the Charleston visitors' bureau, we cross back to the other side of King Street.

"I have no idea where we are, Omar."

"That's kind of the point Claudia." But you're about to be wowed, believe that!

This guy must really be all that, because there is a line

of people coming out of the door and going along the sidewalk. Thanks to Mr. Washington, we don't have to wait. He shops here a lot and knows the owner real well: "I called Jonathan, and it's all set, Omar. He's been keeping up with the protest, and he thinks it's very cool. When you arrive, go to the back door and ring the buzzer. Tell whoever answers that you're my student, and they will let you in," he told me earlier today.

His plan sounds all romantic and whatnot, but I adjust it a little, so I don't reveal to Claudia exactly where we are. I want this to be a complete surprise, homegirl.

We ring the buzzer, and a tall girl with long black-purple hair and oval-shaped glasses answers. I hold up a sheet of paper with the following words written in big black block letters:

I'M OMAR SMALLS.
MR. WASHINGTON SENT US.

She looks at me like I'm the weird one, and then waves us in.

"We're almost there, Claudia," I say, just to reassure her. The store is long and narrow, a hallway with shelves on each wall. It's unlike any other bookstore I've ever been in. Actually, I haven't been in a lot. There's even a gray cat that runs in and out of the tiny rooms off the hallway. When we finally get to the main room, which is just a little bigger than Uncle Al's van, the commotion ratchets up a bit.

People are drinking red wine and talking. A guitarist sits in the corner playing music that I don't recognize and don't particularly care for.

"Nice music," homegirl says.

Uncle Al's van can comfortably seat about nine football players. I've done this a few times. The main room of this bookstore has fifty people crammed into it, and there are another couple hundred lined up outside.

Everybody's here for the author in brown slacks and a tan blazer, signing copies of his latest book. The famous author who goth girl is walking us over to right now. The pale-looking, pudgy, famous author dude who homegirl thinks is the Best. Frickin'. Writer. Ever.

Claudia

Most of my birthdays aren't very memorable. My parents would have a cake, but we didn't really get gifts. I spent most of my birthdays in soup kitchens or in church. They really believed in giving back. I guess when you really get down to it, a birthday is just another day. But out of all of my birthdays, which all seem to just blur together, there is one I will never forget: *this one*.

OMIGOD. "OMIGOD, OMIGOD" is all I can manage to say. "This is not happening."

"I'm afraid it is, young lady," he says to me in a voice that sounds a little like Forrest Gump, if Forrest Gump were a slow-talking college professor. I can't even look at him.

"Pat Conroy just spoke to me," I say to Omar, still not looking at Mr. Conroy. "It's Pat frickin' Conroy."

"Yeah, I know, Claudia. I'm right here with you." When Omar took off the bandanna, I immediately recognized Blue Bicycle Books. My sister's book club gets all their books here.

The summer after sophomore year, I was in a creative writing camp, and we had to read *The Water Is Wide*, a memoir by Pat Conroy.

I borrowed it from the library, like I do most books, in case I don't like them. And thank god I did, because I had some serious problems with it. I mean, I liked his writing, which is why I next read his incredible novel *The Prince of Tides*, but it was clear to me that Mr. Conroy should stick to fiction. When I got over being starstruck, I all but said this to him.

"Mr. Conroy, I am so honored to meet you. I have read all of your books, except the cookbook, which my boyfriend just gave me. This is my boyfriend, Omar," I ramble, putting my hand on his chest to point him out. "You are the best novelist I've read. I even wrote a paper on the tortured low-country souls who populate your books and how Shakespearean your work is. Of course, I wasn't trying to compare you to the *Bard*, but you come pretty close. So

265

here's the thing, and I mean this in the most respectful way possible.

"*The Water Is Wide* is all about YOU. It should have been about THEM. I am sure those children on Daufuskie Island contributed more to their growth and development than your memoir gives them credit for. As much as I applaud your desire to educate them, to teach them how the magic inside books can change their lives for the better, I am struck by your audacity. You were not their salvation. You were not their only hope. If it wasn't you, it might have been someone else, or something else.

"Change is a force, Mr. Conroy. You were an umbrella, an overcoat, perhaps shelter, but you were not the storm that washed away the poor natives' sins. Make no mistake about it, those children, like me, like students in any disadvantaged situation, are very capable of changing their lot.

"With that said, my boyfriend says that the recipes and stories in this new cookbook of yours are awesome. I hope that your memoir skills have improved and are on par with the rest of the book. Would you mind signing?" I hand him the book and then walk around the table to his side. "Omar, take a picture."

* * *

"Wow! I thought he was your favorite author," Omar says to me as we walk back up King Street. We walk through Marion Square arm in arm, the moon our ceiling. We see some kids from school break-dancing on cardboard, parents pushing strollers, and a guy on a blanket reading a book. Glad the Charleston weather came back. This could be a beach night.

"He is!"

"Then why'd you dawg him out like that? You went all bananas on him."

"No, I didn't. I just told him why I thought one of his books was a little suspect. The other twelve are frickin' genius. I mean, if you saw Tim Tebow walking down the street, wouldn't you be real with him?"

"I hate Tim Tebow, but I'm not going off on him just because I think he's overrated."

"See, that's the difference between us, Omar. Claudia Clarke likes to keep it really real—feel me." I tickle him. "Plus he gave me his number. Told me we should grab coffee sometime."

"You don't even drink coffee."

"It's metaphorical, Omar. I'll get tea," I say, laughing. "And what about all the people in there who recognized you from the silent protest. Did you see that one lady with the SHHHHH! T-shirt on?"

"What was really crazy was when we walked outside, and the crowd started clapping and chanting, 'We're fired up, we can't take no mo'.'"

"You're a star on and off the field, babe."

"True dat!"

"Seriously, Omar, this was the sweetest thing anyone has ever done for me. You really got me. Do you treat all your girlfriends like this?"

"Only the ones going to Harvard," he says, and slaps me on the butt. "T-Diddy always does it big."

"Apparently."

"But it ain't over."

"I know," and I kiss him long and hard to let him know how appreciative I am. "Tonight is going to be another very special night for both of us, Omar Smalls."

It gets a little chilly walking up King Street, so Omar drapes me in his leather jacket.

The street is bustling with students from the College of Charleston, all heading to the basketball game against their rivals, Charleston Southern. When we get to George Street, Omar pulls me around the corner. We start walking briskly, like we're on the run. Maybe this is a part of his whole *Mission: Impossible* thing. So mysterious. He pulls me inside an art gallery.

"Omar, what's up?"

"Uh, nothing, I just want to check those, uh, quilts." Yeah, right. If we were playing the free game, the candle would probably die down a little. Maybe he saw a girl he knows, maybe not. Whatever, I'm not going to think about that kind of nonsense on my birthday night. "I'll be right back," he says. "What time is it, Claudia?"

"Six forty-seven."

"We sure are doing a lot of walking tonight."

"Reducing our carbon footprints. T-Diddy is all about going green, homegirl." This makes me laugh.

"These heels are killing me."

"Killing me too, homegirl," he says with that smile, then puts his arm around me, slips his huge palm where my back pocket would be if I had on jeans. Feels great.

"That was a nice quilt exhibit, plus we got to meet the artist. Did you plan this for my birthday, or was it a co-incidence?"

"T-Diddy plans everything. I figured you might have a thing for black mermaids, being that you're all feminist and whatnot."

"I never knew there was such a thing as a black mermaid."

"Hang out with T-Diddy and you might learn a whole lot of new stuff." He lifts me up with ease and hugs me. If I didn't have on this long brown skirt, I'd probably lock my legs around him.

We walk past Blue Bicycle Books again, and the line is even longer now. When we get to the corner, we turn right, and I try to remember which restaurants are down here. I'm eager to know where we're going.

This street is like a little cultural heaven. First, there's a small French bakery that pretty much drags you in with its aroma. Then, there's a Gullah-themed art gallery featuring mainly the works of this artist named Jonathan Green, who once spoke at our school. Next to that is an Italian gelateria that I've never been in. And next to that is our destination. Omar holds the door open for me and ushers me in.

I've heard about Rue de Jean from my parents. They used to go here for their date nights. They raved about the food and how it reminded them of their favorite French restaurant in Montreal. How ironic that I am here for my first real date. This night just keeps on getting better and better.

"Nice choice, Omar."

He winks at me.

"How many in your party?" the hostess asks.

"Deux pour le dinner, *s'il vous plait."* Omar says in a mixture of Brooklyn and Paris, which sends a smile to my face the size of the River Seine. *"Nous célébrons le* birthday *de mon amour."* My heart drops beneath the floor.

Even though the words come out uncomfortably slow. And even though the waitress probably doesn't speak French. LOL! And even though he really didn't have anything to prove, when my boyfriend tells the waitress in Rue de Jean, on my birthday, that I am his *amour*, Omar Smalls has officially TAKEN. ME. THERE. Again.

OMAR

6:47pm

Omar Smalls: Dawg, I just saw them Bayside nuckas on King St. They rolling six deep.

Fast Freddie: Where you at?

Omar Smalls: In an art gallery, near the Sottile

Fast Freddie: Da sottile? WT . . .

Omar Smalls: George Street. Off of King.

Fast Freddie: You hiding out in the water closet?

Omar Smalls: I got homegirl with me.

Fast Freddie: What you wanna do?

Omar Smalls: Text Willie Mack. I'm gonna wait like fifteen minutes. Hurry up.

Fast Freddie: A'ight, if it's going down, we got your back, T. Fo' sho. I'm in the car. I'm in the car w/ B right now. On our way.

Omar Smalls: Thas whas up. Hurry up, we got 7:15 reservations at a French joint, and if we're late, we lose 'em.

Fast Freddie: No hablo espanol. Bwahahaha!

Fast Freddie: What you want us to do when we get there?

Omar Smalls: Make sure them woadies is gone, then text me. Me and homegirl be inside checking out a black mermaid exhibit.

Fast Freddie: Black mermaids? WTFFFFF?

Omar Smalls: Focus man. You coming?

Fast Freddie: Just in case they still downtown and they wanna roll up on you, right?

Omar Smalls: Exactly!!!!

Fast Freddie: T, you still in the water closet?

* * *

Tdiddy Smalls Yesterday was the best day of my life. Be thankful!
Unlike · Comment · Share · Thursday at 1:00 am ·
👍 **You** and **Claudia Clarke** like this.

> **Willie Mack** Dude, you watching Oprah? WTF!!!!
> Thursday at 1:10 am via mobile · Like

> **Blu McCants** Bwahahahahaha!
> Thursday at 1:11 am · Like

> **Claudia Clarke** Y'all leave my babe alone.
> Thursday at 1:11 am · Like

Freddie Callaway "babe" *dead*
Thursday at 1:12 am · Like

Tdiddy Smalls Drinking that haterade.
Thursday at 1:12 am · Like

Savannah Gadsden LOLOLOL!
Thursday at 1:30 am · Like

Claudia Clarke ▶ **Tdiddy Smalls** I can't sleep.
Like · Comment · Share · Thursday at 4:03 am ·

Tdiddy Smalls Me either.
Thursday at 4:05 am via mobile · Like

Claudia Clarke I want to go to Italy.
Thursday at 4:05 am · Like

Tdiddy Smalls *Random*
Thursday at 4:05 am via mobile · Like

Claudia Clarke I just finished reading the two chapters
on Italy, and we have to go.
Thursday at 4:06 am · Like

Tdiddy Smalls I heard the food there is bananas. I'll
take you wherever you want to go.
Thursday at 4:06 am via mobile · Like

Claudia Clarke Awwwwwwwww!
Thursday at 4:06 am · Like

Blu McCants Get a room, already. Jeez!
Thursday at 4:07 am via mobile · Like

RedBone Follow me @RedboneDaRapper
Thursday at 4:10 am · Like

Tdiddy Smalls Oh, wow!
Thursday at 4:10 am via mobile · Like

Blu McCants Bwahahahahahahaha! Only in the country.
Thursday at 4:11 am via mobile · Like

Tdiddy Smalls Claudia, pick up, I'm calling.
Thursday at 4:14 am via mobile · Like

Tdiddy Smalls Ring ring, homegirl.
Thursday at 4:15 am via mobile · Like

Tdiddy Smalls Blu, where ya girl go?
Thursday at 4:23 am via mobile · Like

Tdiddy Smalls Yo, anybody on here?
Thursday at 4:24 am via mobile · Like

RedBone Cop dat Redbone and Hoe Daddy mixtape, playa.
Thursday at 4:25 am · Like

Tdiddy Smalls I love Claudia Clarke like the winter loves snow.

Like · Comment · Share · Thursday at 4:51 am ·

Tdiddy Smalls Homegirl, where you at? Don't make me come over there.

Thursday at 4:51 am via mobile · Like

Freddie Calloway ▶ Tdiddy Smalls T, I tried to call you. Went straight to voicemail. Check your inbox. ASAP.

Like · Comment · Share · Thursday at 4:52 am ·

Tdiddy Smalls Phone's dead. Checking it now.

Thursday at 5:09 am · Like

Blu McCants ▶ Tdiddy Smalls I'm soo sorry . . . but love no longer lives there . . . And no, she didn't supply a forwarding address. . . . Things are changing and so is she . . . asshole

Like · Comment · Share · Thursday at 6:30 am ·

Tami Hill ▶ Tdiddy Smalls Call me boo, if you need a shoulder to lean on.

Like · Comment · Share · Thursday at 7:00 am ·

Belafonte Jones ▶ Tdiddy Smalls T, you coming to school today?

Like · Comment · Share · Thursday at 7:07 am ·

Rich Smalls ▶ Tdiddy Smalls CUZIN, why you ain't tell me

you was 'bout to go all Ray J on these tricks. LOL! #sextape
Like · Comment · Share · Thursday at 7:29 am ·

Eve Chappell via **Kym King** You got exactly what you
asked for. The grass isn't greener on the other side! You had
it good and you wanted "better." . . . Well, Omar, maybe
next time, you will treat the women in your life "better."
Like · Comment · Share · Thursday at 7:51 am ·

* * *

Eve Chappell@EveILLNana: Watch @DaRealTDiddy in the
locker room taking advantage of Kym King. #Busted #SexTape
Click here for video.

"You're an asshole, and she doesn't want to talk to you," Blu
says, and hangs up on me for the fifth time. "EVER!"

Claudia didn't come to school on Friday, so I haven't
seen or spoken to her in four days. I call her back again.

"Look, before you hang up, it wasn't what it looked
like."

"And your clothes magically disappeared and she
poured cement on your dick. And you let her suck . . . you
know what, never mind. You're busted."

"Look, Blu, just tell Claudia I want to talk to her, and I
can expla—" and she hangs up again. She's staying at Blu's

house, but Blu said her brother would shoot me if I showed up at her place. And after hearing the stories about him after he got back from Iraq, I ain't going nowhere near that shell-shocked joker.

Fast Freddie texts me and asks if I want to watch the Jets-Patriots game with him and Belafonte. The only thing I want to do is lie under my covers and pray that Claudia Clarke calls me back and forgives me for this ish that I didn't even really do.

How was I supposed to know that the whole time Kym was pushing up on me in the locker room, Eve was recording everything on her iPhone? That's some foul ish. They set me up, and the messed-up thing is, I didn't even do anything wrong. Not really. It's not like I slept with her.

They made that joint look like I was enjoying it. I mean I was, who wouldn't, but I stopped it. Told her to be out. They made it seem like we did it right there in front of my locker.

I done a lot of messed-up stuff over the years, but Claudia was different. I guess that karma ish is real, 'cause the one time T-Diddy does the right thing is the time he hurts the one girl he loves.

"Smalls, it's your Sunday to cook," Uncle Al says from my doorway. "What are we eating?"

"I don't feel like cooking tonight, Unc."

"Oh, man, you done messed up, didn't you?" he counters, like he's reading the guilt and grief written all over my face. "Didn't I tell you she was special? Dayum, dayum, dayum! What have you gone and done?"

"I made a stupid-ass mistake."

"Watch your mouth, Smalls. So now you're sitting up in this dark room, pouting?"

"She won't even talk to me. I can't even explain to her the truth. I'm in pain, Unc."

"Whatever you did, just give her a few days to work through it all."

"I haven't seen her in four."

"Her clock ain't set by how fast your hands move, Smalls." I don't say anything, just look out my window at the lonely moon. "Write her, tell her your side of things."

"You think that'll work?"

"I still don't know what you did, but it can't hurt." He's right. I take out my phone and start tapping away.

"What's that you doing?"

"You said write her. I'm emailing her."

"That's about the dumbest thing I've ever heard. Smalls, that's not what I meant. Don't email, don't text, don't Twitter, and don't facebutt her."

Whoa, facebutt. Really.

"Write her a real letter, son."

"Like with paper and an envelope?"

"And a stamp and a mailbox." C'mon son. "Put some effort into this. You want her back, don't you? Nothing better than an old-fashioned love letter on some nice parchment paper."

Parchment?

"I got some paper in my printer."

"Just shut up, Smalls. Grab my coat, let's go."

"Where we going, Unc?" I ask, pulling his coat and mine out of the closet.

"Fish tacos," he answers.

Claudia

I haven't written in my journal in over a year. Since Leo broke my heart. I keep playing it over and over in my head. The best birthday of my life. THE WORST BIRTHDAY OF MY LIFE. How did you let this happen, Claudia?

January 27
I am done with love. I've tasted the toxin of hurt.
Swallowed its sword. Love will never be born again.
Because I'm cuttin' the cord.

No matter what I try to do to distract myself—watch TV, read, math homework—I keep getting the same common denominator: Omar Smalls. First, I was at Blu's house, now I'm at my house, locked in my room, listening to the same sad love songs. Why did you let yourself fall like that, so fast? Haven't you learned anything?

January 28
Fourteen Reasons Why I'm Done
Because my heart is in five million pieces
Because my soul is on fire
Because betrayal is like a torch
Because forgiveness is a foreign country
Because I don't have a passport
Because my fears are ocean deep
Because my tears are river wide
Because I met a boy
Because right under the moon, the boy held my hand and promised to show me the light
Because I thought that promises were like mountains, solid and sacred
Because his promises were caves, empty and cold
Because my smile has vanished, my laughter silent
Because life, it seems, is a puzzle
Because I don't know how to put the pieces back together again

I've tried to avoid him in school, but I can't avoid him in my mind. Staring out of the window is my new hobby. He's a guy, Claudia. What did you expect?

January 29

I was really into you, Omar Smalls. A part of me hates you. Letting a guy into my world this fast is unfamiliar. Letting a guy LIKE YOU into my world is unsafe. What you did to me was despicable and horrible, and yes, I too thought "we had a thing." I guess not. A part of me loves the man you could be. Loves how you've changed our school for the better. Made kids care about something. Stood up like a real man is supposed to. How can somebody so wrong be—

"Claudia, open up," my sister screams from the other side of my door. I mute the music. "I know you're not asleep, girl. I heard the music. Don't make me call Mom and Dad." I know she's not doing that, because they'll have like a million things they need her to do. Nice try.

"Well, I know one thing, you're not skipping school again. You have until the morning to get yourself together, or I'm busting the door down. Don't think I won't do it." When I hear her go back down the stairs, I turn my Whitney

Houston back up. "Saving All My Love for You." Jeez!

She's right, I do need to get back to school. AP tests are coming up, and missing a week of class is not good.

Plus I need to come out of my little silent treatment and face the music that awaits me. But I don't care what song he's singing, I'm still not talking to him.

OMAR

Nothing like a sit-down meal at my favorite restautant, Juanita Greenberg's, to brighten up T-Diddy's mood. I probably ate about ten tacos and laughed my butt off. Uncle Al was crackin' jokes all night, had the whole place in stitches.

We get to the van, which is parked right out front, as it always is, in the handicapped spot.

"Oh, snap, I left the keys on the table. Be right back, Unc."

When I run back in to grab them, me and the waitress have a moment. Why not? It ain't like I got a girlfriend anymore. She smiles, I smile. I ask her name, we flirt a little, then, as I'm glancing out the window, I notice a couple of dudes in football jerseys talking to Uncle Al.

"Nice to meet you, Jo. I gotta run, but I'll holla," I tell her, even though I know I probably won't. Claudia's got me vexed.

When I get outside the restaurant, I hear Uncle Al shouting at these kids.

"Like I said, just watch where you spit next time, young 'un!"

"You crippled mutha—"

"Hey, chill on that, homeboy," I say to the kid kirking off on Uncle Al. When he turns around, I know we got trouble. Dayum!

"It's Titty. You with this retard?" says the kid I recognize from the Bayside football team.

"Omar, let's go, before I have to whoop these punks," Uncle Al says. I press the remote to unlock the car. The other Bayside dude, Moose, stands in front of Unc.

"Ty, I guess crip 'bout to get up out that wheelchair," Moose says to his partner, and they laugh.

"Step off—we don't want no trouble, homeboy," I say.

"Well, you found it anyway, Titty," the one named Ty says. "I told you Bayside don't forget."

The loud noise we hear next sounds like a bear stepping on a twelve-inch nail. The few people on the street look at us to see what it is. Ty and I turn around to look, and see Moose on his knees, his arm twisted behind his back and being held by Uncle Al. How in the heck?

When dude turns around, I know he's gonna come at me. I don't let him. As soon as our eyes connect, I clock him, right in the jaw. And he's down. Uncle Al lets Moose go, and he's still moaning on the ground.

"Let's roll, Smalls." I put him in the van, and just like that, we're out.

"What was that about, Smalls?"

"Some ol' nonsense. They're still salty about that beat-down in the championship game."

"That looked like more than a football grudge, Smalls. Some personal beef."

"West Charleston and Bayside been beefing forever, Unc. I don't even sweat it. They got sense enough not to come 'round our way with no craziness."

"I'm just saying be careful. Crazy ain't never made sense."

"What? You sound like Clyfe. Stop worrying, I got you," I say, driving down Meeting Street.

"Just watch your back, son. Uncle Al is straight."

"Yeah, how you get that big joker on the ground like that?"

"I ain't always been in this wheelchair, homeboy. I've

taken down bigger than him."

"That's what's up. When I clocked that kid, he—"

"Smalls, it happened and it's over. I ain't one for glorifying violence and whatnot," he says, like he's about to tell me another long-ass story. Then he stops. Thank you, thank you.

A minute later, the rain comes fast and hard. The silence reminds me of homegirl. I change the subject back to her.

"Uncle Al, I don't even know what to say in a letter. She ain't talked to me in like a week. What am I gonna do?" No answer. "Seriously, dude, I need help, this girl is on my brain."

I peek through the rearview mirror and that joker is asleep. We're fifteen minutes from home and he's out. Juanita Greenberg's does it to him every time.

The radio is broken, but the CD player works. I press play, and one of his slow-jam mix tapes comes on. Nothing like a little Temptations singing "My Girl" to mess you up.

Claudia

I am so sick of petty high school mess. I can't wait to graduate and meet some legitimate men. Heck, and women. This place is just so insignificant. It's like a prison of immaturity with no chance of rehabilitation for any of the frickin' inmates. *I want out!*

Blu and I leave Starbucks, and we're on our way to school.

"I don't know if I can do this, girl. I've never been this embarrassed in my life. He made me look like a two-dollar fool."

"Speaking of that, you still owe me two dollars from last month."

"Really? I'm all distraught and whatnot, and you're cracking jokes?"

"Get over it already. You cried for like three days straight. Stop playing the frickin' victim. Be a woman."

"Thanks for being so sensitive, Blu."

"Uggghh! You act like you still love him." I take a sip of my chai latte and keep my eyes on the road. "If you do, trick, then talk to him."

"Nothing to say. It's gonna take a long time for me to talk to him, and even longer to trust another guy on the planet."

"I heard Uranus had some good guys."

"You're stupid." And we both laugh like we used to, before all the madness started. "As long as I don't have to see him today, ya know."

"I hear ya, girl. But just in case we do, I got my pepper spray."

The first person I see when I walk into school is Omar Smalls. He looks different. It's not like I forgot what he looked like, but I don't see the guy who gave me the best birthday celebration ever. I see the ho. The playa. The guy who bet his friends a hundred fifty dollars that he could sleep with me. I immediately turn and walk down the stairs, past the band room, along the "detention" hallway that goes under the school, and come up the stairs near my government class. Mr. Washington is sitting at his desk.

"We missed you in class on Friday, Ms. Clarke."

"Sorry about that. Rough day. I heard we had a quiz."

"We did, but it was really to make sure everybody's been doing the reading. I know I don't have to worry about you doing the reading." He didn't, normally. But ever since I've been all up in Omar's mix, I haven't been as diligent with all my reading assignments as I should have been. I'll catch up next weekend. Nothing to distract me now.

The bell rings.

On the way to my seat, I get all kinds of sympathy remarks from the students.

"Girl, you okay?"

"That was some messed up ish, Claudia."

"T-Diddy did the same thing to my cousin last year. He's a good football player, but he don't know how to be good to no girls."

When I hear this last comment, I want to come to his defense. Tell her how he came and changed my tire in the middle of the cold night. How he volunteers for Lucky Dog. How he made me a five-course dinner. How he learned French for me. How he introduced me to Pat Conroy.

"Play with fire, and you get burned. I tried to tell you, this here is a big-girl game. Know the rules, bish." I turn

292

around and see Eve walking toward my desk, gritting on me like a pit bull. I sit down and try to ignore her. Don't worry, Claudia. She's not going to touch you; Mr. Washington is right there, up front. She's crazy, but she can't be that stupid.

Turns out she is.

The palm of her hand feels like a hardcover book when it slams against the back of my head. When I hear it hit the floor, I realize it was a book. U.S. history. No she didn't.

I jump up, forgetting the pain momentarily, and instead focus on protecting myself if she tries to come at me.

"Girl, what's your problem. Are you crazy?"

"Oh, yeah, I'm crazy a'ight," she screams, waving her hands all willy-nilly. Where is Mr. Washington? He's got to see this! When Eve steps out of her sandals, a collective "ohhhhhh," fills the class. "Claudia Clarke is about to get a beatdown," somebody hollers.

She comes at me fierce and fast, her long and flaming-red-fingernailed hands flailing in the air, and before I know it, I'm back in tae kwon do camp. Sixth grade. I only made it to yellow belt, and the only thing I learned was how to block and punch. I've never tried it outside of the white uniform. Until today. I'm Claudia Clarke, the good girl. So when I block her wild blow with my left arm, and my right fist connects with her face like a hammer, everyone is in shock. Especially me. She slides to the floor like a holy roller in church. I drop my books, ready to do it again once she gets up.

"Who's burned now, bish?" I scream at her, feeling like I've discovered the Pam Grier in me. It feels kinda great. But before I can stomp on her, or whatever two years of martial arts and six years of pent-up, raw, unadulterated, pure hatred of her was dictating me to do, Mr. Washington separates us. Now he shows up.

"Stop it this minute, both of you."

"Both of us?" Eve says, standing up. "She's the one who punched me." I see blood dripping from her hand, which is covering her eye, and I feel a little bad. Only a little.

Mr. Washington instructs a couple of students to take Eve to the nurse's office—before he realizes that there is no nurse's office. It got cut in last year's budget deficit.

I run and get the first-aid kit and give it to Mr. W.

"Even a prison has a nurse," he screams. "This damn school is worse than a prison. Shit! Shit! Shit!"

"Well, it's a good thing you don't have to be locked up in here anymore," says a voice behind us. Standing in the doorway is Principal Jackson, aka Cruella, and some young white dude in a corduroy suit who none of us recognize.

"Uh, Dr. Jackson, we're all just a little discombobulated. What can I help you with?" Mr. Washington asks, still treating Eve, who is, justifiably, still gritting on me.

"Actually, there is nothing you can help me with. Is that blood? Was someone fighting in here, Mr. Washington?" The room grows quieter than it was before.

"There was no fight. Eve just, um, stumbled on her way to her desk and hit the corner of the desk. It was ugly." Eve looks at me and I know she won't say anything, because Cru has a rule that fighting is an automatic one-week suspension, whether you're the fighter or the fightee. So we both keep quiet.

"She fell on her eye?" Dr. Jackson asks suspiciously. "Oh, never mind, just have some of your students get it cleaned up."

"Will do."

"In the meantime, can you step out in the hallway for a minute, Mr. Washington? There is something we need to discuss." The entire class stares at Dr. Jackson and then at Mr. Washington.

"I'm a little busy here. As soon as I finish, I'll come down to your office," he responds.

"Unacceptable. Don't make this harder than it needs to be. I need to speak with you this moment." Mr. W ignores her, still tending to evil Eve's busted eye.

"Fine. Someone get some ice from the cafeteria," he says to no one in particular, while shooting me a disappointed look. He hands the first-aid kit to another student. I head for the cafeteria, and he follows Cruella into the hallway. While I'm walking away, I can hear snippets of their conversation: ". . . insubordination . . . the school board voted . . . so many complaints about you . . ."

I do hear Mr. Washington's response loud and clear.

"Bullshit," he yells. Something's going down, and it's not good. I grab the ice and run back to class. I see Cruella talking to another teacher, and the white guy in the corduroy suit standing outside the door. Inside, Mr. Washington is talking to the class:

"I'm being laid off. A substitute will take over class until they reassign one of the existing teachers to this class."

"No way, Mr. W," says one student.

"That's ill—how long before you leave?" asks another.

"I have fifteen minutes to exit the building. The guy standing in the hall is my escort."

I run outside and see Dr. Jackson walking away. "This isn't fair," I yell. She whips her head around so fast, it takes a second for her body to catch up.

"Ms. Clarke, I've had about enough of you and your

antics these past few weeks. If I were you, I'd keep quiet."

"I will not," I say defiantly. This is not the best week, and it's the worst frickin' day to try to silence me. Oh hells no!

"Well then, you can pack your proverbial bags also, because you're suspended for the day. Want to try for two?"

Before I tell her hell yeah, I hear a loud commotion from Mr. Washington's room. I rush back inside.

"Hey, check this out. Kids are leaving." Leaving?

"Yeah, they're all walking onto the lawn."

Cruella apparently followed me, because she rushes over to the window. Several students follow. Mr. Washington and I, and the rest of the class, go over as well, and sure enough, there's got to be a hundred students outside, and more are coming. What's going on?

"Oh, snap, y'all, I just checked FB on my phone," Tami hollers. "Listen to this: 'The governor and her flunkies on the school board didn't take us serious. They just fired a bunch of our favorite teachers. Let's show them how we do. Meet me on the lawn. Not later. Not tomorrow. Now. ASAP. Oh, it's going down. Speak up now!'"

"Who wrote that, Ms. Hill?" Cru asks with a stern look.

But Tami doesn't need to answer, because everybody knows who wrote it. And when we look out the window at the guy standing on top of a picnic bench, it's confirmed. There he is, looking like Dr. Martin frickin' Luther King in jeans and Timberlands, standing on the mountaintop. Within seconds, our class is empty.

Damn you, Omar Smalls.

OMAR

I pop a few more sunflower seeds in my mouth, take a swig of Mountain Dew, and put both back inside my locker.

"YoT-DiddyThereIsYourGirlComingInTheDoor."

"Where?" I turn around quick, and sure enough, homegirl is in the hallway. I shoot past Fast Freddie and Willie Mack, and about twenty other people, like I'm running down the sidelines toward the end zone. Unfortunately, I see Cru barking in the hallways like she does every morning. The wicked witch has already got it in for me, and I know I better stop running before I get ISS.

This is my chance to talk to her, see if she read the letter I left on her windshield.

I briskly walk past Dr. Jackson, avoiding eye contact,

but by the time I get to the school's entrance, Claudia is gone. I look behind me, in front of me, to the side, outside, but there is no sign of her.

Even though I'm standing in the middle of my school, in the middle of the school that I put on the map. Even though I'm *that dude*, I feel lost.

The bell rings, and I'm frozen.

"YoTWhere'dSheGo? YouA'ight?"

"Let's go" is all I can say, as we head to class.

As Fast Freddie, Willie Mack, and I pass the library, I see Dr. Jackson coming out of our class, heading in the opposite direction. She's smiling, for once. Still, I slow my pace, so I won't run into her. Ms. Stanley, the librarian, stumbles out of the library with her coat on, crying, barely able to hold the box she's carrying.

"Let me get that for you, Ms. Stanley." I take it from her and hand it to Fast Freddie. "You okay?"

"I'm okay."

"ThenWhyYouCyring?"

"T-Diddy, the school board bootlegged us. They just pink-slipped Ms. Stanley and a whole bunch of teachers," Luther runs up to us and says.

"They laid us—" Ms. Stanley says, still unable to get out a whole thought without bawling.

"Oh *hell* no," I say, like I'm in the huddle and we're down. "Ms. Stanley, keep your head up. We got you! Fred, Luther, let's roll."

"WhatWeDoingKid?"

"It's going down today, believe that. Pull out your phones." We're not supposed to have phones in school, but everybody has them—in pockets, in backpack secret compartments, in bras. I pull mine from my sock. "It's overtime, people. First they take our band, our music, now they take our favorite teachers. What's next, they gonna cancel lunch to save money?"

"What's the plan, Omar?" Luther asks. I have no idea what we're going to do, but I know that we aren't going to allow Cru and these clueless school board people to mess with our futures anymore. Where did all these people in the hallway come from?

"Meet me out on the lawn right now! Tweet it, post it, text it, scream it. Put the word out. We are going to turn this mutha out. Y'all feel me." Judging by the commotion and loud applause in the hallway, they do. Fingers are tapping away on cell phones. Everybody's spreading the word. Oh, it's definitely going down.

"LEGGGGOOO!" screams Fast Freddie, and everyone in the hallway heads outside. The word gets around fast, because students are already outside, before us. Oh yeah, it's on now.

Outside, the weather is perfect for whatever it is we're about to get into. Sunny and almost seventy degrees; this Charleston weather is as fickle as a Brooklyn bus schedule.

Half the school is outside. I know Cru and her staff must be tripping right about now. And more students are exiting the building. It's pep-rally crazy out here, and now I have to figure out what the plan is. I jump up on a picnic bench and glimpse a sea of West Charleston faces in front of me. Getting antsy, they holler and scream.

"WHAT WE GONNA DO, T-DIDDY?"

"WE FIRED UP!"

"WHY DID THEY FIRE THE TEACHERS?"

"I THOUGHT WE WON THE SILENT PROTEST!"

I scan the crowd and see Fast Freddie and Willie Mack right in front, Blu talking to Luther, kids in SHHHHH! T-shirts. But I don't see homegirl. Last time I did this, she was up here with me. C'mon, son, you got this.

The crowd quiets down and everyone looks at me, waiting for their marching orders.

"Those who want freedom, and yet fear agitation" is how I begin, because I remember Clyfe saying it yesterday, although the word he used wasn't "fear," it was "deprecate," but none of these jokers probably know what it means. Heck, I don't even know. "They are men and women who want crops without plowing the ground, they want rain without thunder and lightning, They want the ocean without the roar of the waters," I shout. The ocean. Remember the ocean, T?

"Preach!" somebody screams from the crowd.

"It's about to be a storm up in here," hollers somebody else.

"That'sMyDawg!" screams Fast Freddie.

"Y'all feel me." I'm getting amped, right along with the students. Oh yeah, it's on now.

"We tried to be quiet, but they didn't hear us. So now we're gonna get in their faces. We're gonna get loud," I say, and that's when the idea hits me.

Uncle Al once told me about the time when he was a student at Howard University and the students staged a sit-in protest in the administration building. They were protesting the expulsion of like thirty-eight students. I don't remember what for, but I do remember they occupied the administration building and they won.

"The school board wants to disrupt our education with a bunch of bullshit moves, then let's disrupt their ish. We're taking our fight to their front door."

The roar makes the ground tremble, which makes the picnic table wobble. These kids are fired up fo' sho.

"How are we gonna get there, Omar?"

"We're gonna march, like they used to do in the old days," I answer, feeling like I'm on a mission and can't nobody break my stride.

"Walk?" screams somebody from the crowd, and then all kinds of moans and groans start.

"That's like ten miles, dawg."

"Ain't nobody trying to march ten miles."

I admit I hadn't really thought the whole marching thing through. I don't even run three in practice.

"I'm driving my truck! Who wants a ride?" yells a kid from the back of the crowd.

"A'ight, that's what's up. It's not about the march anyway. Y'all get there however. Just meet me on the steps of the school board building in like twenty minutes. LEGG-GOO!"

Kids start dispersing. I jump down and make my way over to Fast Freddie and Willie Mack.

"Willie, can you drive?"

"You got gas money?"

"WeTryingToPlanARevolutionAndThisWoadieTalking-AboutGas!"

"C'mon, son, I got you. Let's do this."

We make our way over to Willie's Honda and jump in. Actually, we don't jump in just yet, because we have to push-start that baby. When we get it moving, we all jump in.

"T, this ain't no innocent school-type ish anymore. We're about to break the law."

"IGotYourBackButYouSureWeWantToDisturbThe-Peace."

I wasn't so sure when I said it, but looking in the side-view mirror, I know I'm doing the right thing. There, driving her latchkey car, following us, is homegirl.

I have never been so sure about anything in my life.

Claudia

Channel7News@7News: Omar Smalls, W. Charleston HS take over Administration building: See video <u>here</u> #7News #SilentTreatment

It's got to be at least a thousand people out here. But only half are from our school. I've seen kids I recognize from other bands: Burke, Mount Pleasant, even Bayside. It's almost six o'clock, which means we've been out here for nine hours. With all the chanting, singing, talking, and laughing, and the barrage of TV reporters interviewing any and everybody, the time has gone by pretty quick, though. Still, I can feel the evening chill coming.

There's twelve of us, lined up in front of the building doors, locked arm in arm. One of the reporters from

News Channel Seven called us the Panther Twelve. Omar is on one end, I'm on the other. I still haven't spoken to him. Everyone else is seated on the steps, on cars, across the street in the park, in trees, everywhere but in the street, where the armed cops are directing traffic and waving their batons and pepper-spray containers. I'm convinced that the only reason they haven't bum-rushed us is because of the dozens of newspaper and TV people swarming the protest.

Not a single school board member has shown up to acknowledge us, address our demands. Granted, they can't get out the front door, because we're blocking it, but I'm sure there are other ways to exit the building. A lot of teachers are here, and not just from our school. The coolest thing is that a lot of local celebrities and community people have stopped by to show us love.

Still, I wonder how much longer everyone will last, with the weather changing and no food. My stomach has growled a few times. I bet you the school board people think we're going to get too tired or hungry to keep this up. I hope they're wrong.

When Omar wasn't looking at me, one time while he was being interviewed, I looked into his eyes, and for the first time in many days, I saw a glimpse of the guy I was starting to really like.

Don't get me wrong, I'm still pissed. Mainly at myself, for trusting him, for believing that he could be anything more than a football-playing hustler. He wrote me some sappy love letter, but I'm not playing the fool twice.

Without you, my world is damp and dark, Claudia. At night I walk on wet sand, tumbling toward your arms. But you are not there. I cannot find breathing room outside your arms. Until you talk to me, I am waiting to exhale. . . . You make me want you to kidnap me. On a beach. At midnight, hands bound, perfect. Lips held captive by lips. . . . I am sorrier than sorry. I am lost in this darkness. Come back, light. Come back!

Yadda, yadda, yadda. No way he wrote that. I may forgive him eventually, but I will never forget. That ship done sank, homeboy.

"Girl, if SWAT comes out of the back that truck, I'm outta here," Blu says at seven thirty, pointing to a big white truck that the cops let pull up in front of the sit-in.

"No way that's SWAT. This is West Charleston, not Beijing," I answer, trying to convince myself more than her.

"I'm just saying, remember what they did to those students out in California."

"Hey, everybody hold tight, something's about to go down," Omar shouts, and we lock arms even tighter. We make eye contact for the first time since my birthday. He mouths something to me, but I don't acknowledge him. And then I hear somebody down near the truck calling my name.

"Is there a Claudette Clarke here?" says the pudgy guy exiting the truck. I'm not being arrested, unless police now wear shorts, a T-shirt, and flip-flops. Several people sitting on the steps near him point to us. The guy starts walking toward me.

"If he pulls out a pepper-spray can, I'm knocking his ass out and running. You with me?" Blu whispers.

I nervously laugh as the guy approaches us.

"Who's Claudene Clarke?" he says.

"What do you want with her?" Omar says, breaking the line and walking toward me.

"Special delivery. They told me to ask for, uh—"

"It's Claudia Clarke," I say, correcting this dude who is no more SWAT than I am.

"Okay, cool, I just need you to sign this." He shoves a piece of paper at me.

"Don't do it," Blu screams. "Could be anthrax on that

receipt!" Sometimes Blu can be insane in the membrane.

"Chill, Blu, I got this," I tell her.

"We're kind of in the middle of something, mister," Omar says to the guy.

"Sir, you can give whatever it is you have to me, thank you," I say, letting Omar know that I no longer need him to come to my rescue.

"You may need some help with this, Ms. Clarke. It's a pretty big delivery. Here, this is the note that goes with the order," fat dude says. He hands me an envelope and heads down to his truck.

"Be careful opening it," Blu says. I roll my eyes at her. Most of the Panther Twelve, except Omar, Blu, and me, are still locked down. A few kids from the steps have come up to see what all the commotion is about.

"Hey, look," Belafonte hollers, pointing at the big U-Haul truck. "It's eating time." He and a few others break the line. Omar, Blu, and I look at the truck in complete shock, then immediately get back in formation so we can keep the doors blocked.

Pudgy dude is passing out pizza boxes, from Monza, Sabatini's, and Mellow Mushroom. Even though these are the most bougie pizza joints in Charleston, the kids are grabbing them like it's spring water in the desert.

I open the expensive-looking envelope. And read aloud what's printed on the cream-colored note card.

> I know you don't need my help,
> But even the natives have to eat. . . .
> P. Conroy

For a split second, I try not to laugh. I don't want Omar feeling that I've let my guard down. But I have, and I do, and he does too, and everybody who heard the note looks at us like we're loons.

In all the excitement, I fail to notice the change in position in the Panther Twelve line. Blu is now next to Luther Lee, who's in the middle. Standing next to me, locked arm in arm like we've just walked down the aisle, is none other than Omar Smalls, smiling like he's about to score.

Now, I want to sleep. After eating three slices of pizza, I have caught the itis.

It's eight o'clock when the poet laureate of South Carolina shows up with a bunch of her writer friends. They saw us on the news and they really believe in what we're doing and they want to show support and yadda yadda yadda.

The pretty poet lady asks us can she read a poem to

the group. Omar looks at me, and I nod. I'm ambivalent, because on the real, we're already tired, and the last thing we need is for pretty poet lady to read us some poem that nobody understands.

Omar hollers at the protesters, dwindled in number to about two fifty after dinner, and wakes a lot of them up. He introduces pretty poet lady, who looks so small standing next to him. He stands back in line, and the crowd, most of whom are this close to going back to sleep anyway, give her their attention.

She begins like this: "'Keeping Quiet' by Pablo Neruda. 'Now we will count to twelve/and we will all keep still. . . .'" And, with these few words she has my attention. When she says, "'Life is what it is,'" Omar and I look at each other.

It's like this poem is for us. It's for me. It's for Omar. It's for West Charleston High School, it's for students everywhere who are tired of being treated as invisible, as unspoken, as unheard. More students pay attention now, and this small pretty poet lady has a voice of a hundred lions.

And then she starts counting, measured and assured.

And with each number, students begin to stand up, and raise their hands, counting in silence. Some students are holding up their iPhones, displaying their candelight apps. This is better than the best frickin' concert I've ever been to.

I have no idea where we're going with this, but I am compelled to take my arm from inside Omar's and raise mine too. So I do it. He raises his also, and when she gets to seven, Omar's powerful hand clasps mine. I let it stay there. I have no idea what this means, but it feels right. I have no idea what any of us will do when we get to twelve. I never find out.

The doors behind us open.

"Step aside, step aside," says the cop in front. Behind him are Mayor Deal, Superintendent Rooney, Cruella, Dr. Gwen Hinton, my old middle school teacher who's now on the school board—she winks at me—and, surprisingly, her majesty, our governor. Whoa, this should be interesting.

Dr. Jackson rolls her eyes at me. I curse her out in French. In my mind. And then kind of laugh to myself. Omar looks at me, and still having not spoken to him, I just shrug.

"We're fired up, can't take no mo'," he says. Then, he says it again, louder. Blu joins him. Then the poet woman starts hollering it, and before long, the whole crowd is chanting.

"Okay, okay, let's calm down. The governor has a few

things to say." This directive from the mayor only makes us yell it louder. Cruella whispers something to Omar. He looks at me, then stops chanting and puts his finger in front of his mouth.

"Shhhh!" he says to the crowd, and everyone follows the leader.

"Thank you," the governor begins. "For your consideration, and for your passion. Here in South Carolina, we aim to bring out the best in our students. We educate you because we want you to make something of yourselves, to play a significant role in the betterment of our society, not just here in Charleston, but across this beautiful globe of ours."

Globe, really? Jeez!

"You students have exercised your democratic principles, and while I can't reward your specific actions, your community I'm sure respects you. You have made your point. I've received calls from worried and angry parents. Your peers from other schools around the state have called to express support for your concerns. I'm sorry I couldn't get here earlier, but Mr. Rooney and Dr. Jackson and I had to sit down and discuss your demands.

"Today, a school board meeting was called by Dr. Hinton, and they have proposed new legislation that will allocate some discretionary funds to keep a few more of your arts classes and reinstate all ninety-five teachers from your city who were laid—"

She can't even say the word "off" before the crowd goes frickin' bananas! Kids are whistling, throwing empty pizza boxes in the air, hugging, barking, high-fiving each other, screaming *"YEAH"* at the top of their lungs. I look at Omar, expecting a full-on smile to match mine, but his eyes are focused on something in the crowd.

"Okay, calm down kids. I know this is good news, but let's not cause a ruckus," Superintendent Rooney exclaims.

I look in the direction of where Omar is looking and I see some guys in Bayside jackets body dancing like they're at a rock concert. It looks like the kids they're slamming against aren't too appreciative. But this isn't what's got my eye.

"Now we're going to ask you all to go home. The protest is over; your demands have been met. Let's all go home and have a peaceful end to the night," Rooney continues.

I didn't see them at the rally, and I sure didn't expect to see them here, but walking my way like they're a gang of two are Kym and Eve. I glance over at Blu, but she and the rest of the Panther 12 are already being escorted down the steps by the police.

"I'm going to ask all police officers to help us clear the

area. Good night, students," the superintendent adds, then follows the governor and the rest of the delegation back inside.

"I told you it wasn't over, bish," says Eve, her eye black and blue and swollen like a rotten peach.

"Ain't no bitches around here, Eve, why you trippin'?" Omar says, and I notice for the first time that we're still holding hands.

"I got this" are my first words to Omar. "Look, Eve, I'm sorry for hitting you. That was wrong and immature. And Kym, I don't have beef with you. I'm willing to squash, if you are." I've had a lot of time to think these past four days, and I realize that I may be a little snobby and arrogant and yadda yadda yadda.

"You ain't special, trick. I had him—now what," Kym says. Did you not hear what I just said? Jeez!

"Now what? Well, now you go back to your pitiful, fake, unfulfilling, odious life, and me and my man will go off into the night. Bish." What can I say, I'm a work in progress. I got so caught up in the word "odious" and that she probably didn't know what it meant that the whole "my man" thing just kind of slipped out.

"Titty is the only bitch I see," says one of the Bayside boys I saw body-slamming earlier. He passes a brown paper bag to another guy, who chugs it.

"Yeah, what you gonna do now, quarterblack?" the other says, reaching into his coat pocket. Omar lets my hand go.

"Claudia, get outta here. Run," he says. Eve and Kym swing on me at the same time. Kym connects with my ear, and it hurts like hell. I see Willie Mack bum-rush one of the Bayside boys, and like a slow-motion movie, Eve comes at me all wild style. Omar tries to block her, but he gets hit with the brown paper bag.

"Police!" is the next-to-last thing I hear. The gunshot is the last.

OMAR

When I was twelve, me and some of my friends used to play streetball. We called ourselves the Presidents. We weren't very original, seeing as how we lived on President Street.

In Brooklyn, every block had its own team, and we played on Sundays. Well, this one particular Sunday, we were playing a group of kids from Nostrand Avenue, over on their street. Me and my friend Malcolm couldn't understand why they wanted to play us again, given that we'd squashed them twice already.

So we're in the middle of the game, beating them again. I think the score was like 21 to 7, and we were about to score again. While we're in the huddle, I see one of their guys kneel down behind the wheel of a car on the street and pick up a gun. I yell, "GUN!" and my whole squad turns around and looks, when what we should have done was run. The dude points the gun in our direction and fires. That's when we take off running. Everybody except Malcolm.

When I turn back to look, the guy who fired and the rest of his team are running in the opposite direction, and Malcolm is on the ground holding his arm and screaming. Blood is shooting out from it all over the ground. I run over to him and ask what I should do. He looks me in the eye, crying, and asks, "Omar, am I dying?"

Some old lady comes out of her house with a rag that she ties around his arm, which makes him scream more. A few minutes later, a couple police cars show up, and an ambulance. This was the first time somebody I knew, somebody close to me, was ever shot.

Today was the second.

I see the doctor walking toward the waiting room, which is filled with a bunch of Panthers and her family. I intercept him before he gets here.

"Is she okay?" I ask. "Is she alive?"

"I need to see the family first, young man," he responds.

"Doctor, I need to know that she's okay," I say. He walks

319

past me into the waiting room. Everyone jumps up when they see him.

"Is the family here?" Why does he keep asking for the family? Is he going to tell them that she's dead? The doctor walks over to her family. I follow him, as do a lot of kids.

"She's going to be okay. She's stable. Luckily the bullet went in and out. Let's let her rest; the surgery was a little taxing on her body."

"OmarKym'sGonnaBeFine," Fast Freddie says

"It's my fault. They were after me. It's my fault."

"It's those goons' fault," Willie Mack says. "Let's get some air, dude. Give her family some space."

We walk outside the hospital, and I see homegirl coming our way.

"Fellas, give me a sec," I say. I just want to hug her. So I do, only she doesn't really hug me back.

"You all right?" she asks. Maybe she still cares.

"I'm good . . . you? That could have been you, Claudia. I'm so sorry," I say, and try to hug her again, unable to hold back the tears. "If you had been shot, I would be in jail right now, 'cause I woulda kilt them all."

"Killed, not kilt," she says, and smiles.

"Look, I'm sorry about the whole Kym craziness. I've been trying to tell you for like a week."

"I got your fifty messages and your emails and your letter."

"So we good?" I say, sniffling. She hands me a tissue.

"No, Omar, we're not good."

"I said I'm sorry. I mean it. It was a mistake."

"It was more than a mistake. You betrayed me. You played me. Sorry doesn't cut it when you say you're feeling me, and the next thing I know, your supposed ex-girlfriend is going down on you," she says, a little too loud.

"I didn't mean to hurt you, Claudia," I say.

"No one ever means to hurt you, but they do. I'm just gonna need some time to get over this, Omar." She hands me another tissue. "T-Diddy's crying in public. Let me get my camera out."

"Oh, so now you got jokes," I say, in between sobs.

"On the bright side, we did it."

"Yeah, I guess we did. This semester has been kind of out of control."

"Kind of? Try *way out of control*," Claudia says.

"At least the teachers got their jobs back, and we got some of the arts funding back." Finally, a smile.

"You going inside?" She doesn't answer, just stares at me like she wants to say something. This may be a moment. Our moment.

"Is it wrong that I want to kiss you right now, Claudia Clarke?" I say, getting some of my swagger back.

"Not wrong at all, but it's not happening," she counters.

"What about tomorrow?" I say.

"You should just be glad I'm finally speaking to you," she answers, walking past me and into the hospital.

I love you, Claudia Clarke.

Claudia

Claudia Clarke It's Complicated.

Like · Comment · Share · 30 minutes ago ·

    Tdiddy Smalls Bonjour mademoiselle
    Wednesday at 9:34 pm · Like

    Claudia Clarke I'm studying for Mr. W's test tomorrow.
    You should be too.
    Wednesday at 9:34 pm · Like

    Tdiddy Smalls I was just wondering if you're coming to
    see me play at Miami.
    Wednesday at 9:39 pm · Like

    Claudia Clarke #random
    Wednesday at 9:39 pm · Like

323

Tdiddy Smalls I'm serious.
Wednesday at 9:39 pm · Like

Claudia Clarke If y'all play Harvard, sure
#CrimsonTide
Wednesday at 9:40 pm · Like

Tami Hill Claudia, I just want you to know, I ride with
you. Me and Eve don't get down like that anymore
#PantherDance
Wednesday at 9:40 pm · Like

Freddie Calloway Hole up, how y'all be getting down,
for real.
Wednesday at 9:40 pm · Like

Willie Mack ROFL!
Wednesday at 9:40 pm · Like

Claudia Clarke Y'all silly. Thx Tami.
Wednesday at 9:40 pm · Like

Blu McCants T-Diddy crazy in love.
Wednesday at 9:40 pm · Like

Belafonte Jones Word.
Wednesday at 9:41 pm · Like

Tdiddy Smalls Why y'all up in here?
Wednesday at 9:42 pm · Like

Blu McCants Don't make it easy on him, girl.
Wednesday at 9:44 pm · Like

Tdiddy Smalls Haters.
Wednesday at 9:44 pm · Like

Freddie Calloway Word.
Wednesday at 9:44pm · Like

Tami Hill Great idea! Anybody wanna play words w/ friends?
Wednesday at 9:45 pm · Like

Freddie Calloway Bwahahahahahaha!
Wednesday at 9:45 pm · Like

Blu McCants Only in the country.
Wednesday at 9:45 pm · Like

Tdiddy Smalls Claudia, I'm calling you, pick up.
Wednesday at 9:46 pm · Like

Claudia Clarke Told you, I'm busy. What's up?
Wednesday at 9:49 pm · Like

Tdiddy Smalls You got some candles I can borrow?
Wednesday at 9:50 pm · Like

Claudia Clarke Bwahahahahahaha! Whatever, Omar. Bye.
Wednesday at 9:55 pm · Like

"Uncle Al wants to know if you want to come over for dinner on Sunday."

"He does not. That's all you. You're not slick, Omar."

"I'm glad you decided to come to the party with me, Claudia."

"I didn't come with you. I met you here. Don't get it twisted—this is not a date, homeboy."

"Dang, Claudia Clarke is hard-core. It's been like a month. Give me a break."

"Did that once. How'd that work out for me?"

"I'm just saying. T-Diddy got that Mary J. Blige real love for you, homegirl."

"Be happy we're friends."

"Oh, we're back to that."

"It is what it is."

"I've been thinking about the metal detectors. We should do something, Claudia." Even though the only gun at the sit-in was owned by a student from Bayside, Cruella decided that we should have metal detectors in our school, to protect us. From us.

"This is your new strategy to get me back. Another protest. Be original."

"This ain't about you. It's about the people. Fightin' back. Galvanizing the streets," Omar says, smiling.

"You got a plan?"

"C'mon, T-Diddy always got a plan," he says, and grabs my hand. "I'm not sure I can trust you though. Seems that Robert Smalls was a frickin' Republican." I pull my hand away.

"A Republican? Really?"

"A congressman from the great state of South Carolina."

"I wonder how he found time to do that, when he was so busy Saving. The. Frickin'. Union."

"Good point." We both laugh.

"Ya know, I really don't want to do this tonight," he says.

"What? Omar Smalls, aka T-Diddy, aka Panty Dropper, aka Used to Be My Man, doesn't want to stay at a house party and get his freak on. C'mon, lover, they're about to do the T-Diddy Shuffle. More bounce to the ounce, remember?"

"Still with the jokes."

"I'm hungry," I say.

"True. Let's go out for dinner," he says. "We can go to

Alluette's. Some dude named Charleston is playing tonight. I know how much you like jazz." Actually, it's Charlton, as in Charlton Singleton, the slickest frickin' trumpet player in Chucktown. At least he's trying.

"I'm down with that. But I'm really feeling like some Juanita Greenberg's. The fish tacos are the bomb." He just stares at me with the whole curly-lip smile thing. One thing I've learned these past few weeks is that silence doesn't mean we have run out of things to say, only that we are trying not to say them. Then he hugs me. His chest is hard and cozy.

"I miss you. I love you, and I'm sorry," he whispers in my ear. I want to collapse in Mr. Football's arms. Instead, I punch Mr. Football in his arm, changing the mood quickly, for my own sake.

"Let's roll, homeboy."

"I'll get you back, believe that," he says. "Or I'll die trying."

"Magnolia Cemetery's nice. I'm sure they have a nice one in Beaufort, too."

"That's just wrong, homegirl." We both laugh. "You ready, silly?"

"One thing we have to do first," I reply.

I lead him over to the kitchen, where Willie Mack and

Freddie Callaway are drinking some suspicious-looking pink liquid.

"WhatUpY'all."

"I hope you don't need my car again, dawg," Willie Mack says.

"Naw, man. I'm good," Omar says.

"BongBong," Freddie Callaway says, and starts laughing.

"So I'm a nasty girl now, huh, Fred?" Freddie Callaway looks like he just got caught stealing a grape Popsicle. Omar and Willie Mack laugh, but Fast Freddie is not amused.

"I think you two owe T-Diddy something," I say to both of them. The boys look perplexed. "A buck fifty, I think it was." I reach inside the pocket of T-Diddy's jacket, which I still have from when he fixed my tire. I pull out a pair of lace-trimmed red panties.

The look on their faces, mouths scraping the floor, eyes all bugged out, is priceless.

"It's all about the Benjamins, baby," I add, and drop the brand-new, never-worn silk panties Blu gave me two Christmases ago in front of them.

"OhSnapWillieDidSheJustDropThePanties?"

"You heard what the lady said. Y'all woadies better have my loot on Monday," Omar says.

"Where you going, T? The party just started," Willie Mack hollers.

"C'mon, son, you know how T-Diddy gets down," Omar adds, doing the whole curly-lip thing.

"Thong thong!" I holler, grabbing his arm, both of us cracking up beneath the silver moon.